A Brighter Fear

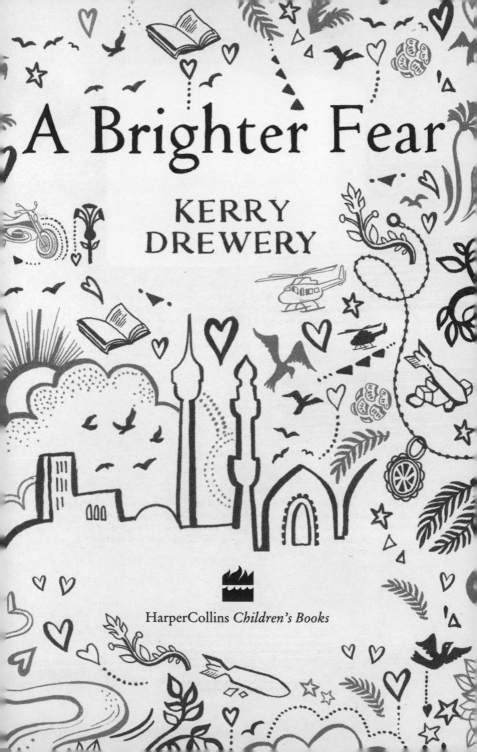

A Brighter Fear

KERRY DREWERY

HarperCollins *Children's Books*

First published in paperback in Great Britain by HarperCollins *Children's Books* 2012
HarperCollins *Children's Books* is a division of HarperCollins*Publishers* Ltd
77–85 Fulham Palace Road, Hammersmith, London W6 8JB

The HarperCollins Children's Books website is
www.harpercollins.co.uk

1

Copyright © Kerry Drewery 2012

ISBN: 978-0-00-744657-5

Printed and bound in the UK by
Clays Ltd, St Ives Plc

To Russ and to Dad, with love.
To PH, with thanks for listening... and listening...
And to Karen and Sally, with fond memories of
so many cups of coffee drunk and
too many chip baguettes eaten.

BEFORE THE BEGINNING

I am Luisa. I am Amira. I am Maysoon, Fay, Samara.

I am black. I am white. I am Asian.

I am Sunni, Shia, Christian.

I am Arab, Persian, Jew, Iraqi.

I am Mesopotamia. I am a million.

I am everyone. I am Baghdad.

I want to tell you my story, yet I want you to

hear everyone's. Mine is not unusual, it is not special.

So many the same: the difference only a name,

a job, a family, a religion.

A million voices, a million stories.

And I am one.

My name is Lina.

AUTHOR DREWERY, KERRY

TITLE A BRIGHTER FEAR   13+

NB. C400 475 410

Date	Name
30.1.17	cazzie mcclure 85
13-12-14.	Jersey magill 8r

CHAPTER ONE

Baghdad, March 2005

Before the war, fear hung over everyone, and we all knew that even voicing our true opinions was dangerous.

Although it was one threat, one regime, there were a million eyes and ears looking out over every city and town and street and home, ready to hear that one wrong word spoken, or that one wrong opinion offered. By anyone.

Before the war, before the Americans in 2003 with their bombs, I couldn't have spoken like this, because even thinking like this was impossible if you wanted to live, if you didn't want to disappear. As my dear Mama discovered.

Fear was never discussed, because fear was constant;

you lived in it and it lived in you.

Back then, before the war and the madness it brought, my papa would've been shocked to hear me speak like this. He would've taken hold of me, I'm sure, scared for the life of his only child, clasped his hand to my mouth, his finger to his lips, his eyes wide with panic. But I knew, as all Iraqis of sound mind did, the importance of muted opinions and quiet anonymity, and the memory of how things were lies only just beneath the surface, even now.

Years of living like that are difficult to change, and I pause to remember that back then, merely what I've already spoken about would've been of interest to the Mukharabat, the secret police; that they would've found reason to arrest me, torture me, kill me even.

And so Iraqis spoke in silence, and to hear them, to really *hear* what they thought, what they felt, you needed to listen not to what they said, but to what they didn't say.

Now? I shake my head. Now, one threat has been replaced by many. Uncontrolled and uncontrollable. Each with its own opinions and wishes and aspirations for the future.

What do I want for my future? I hear you ask. Is it

survival? Or dare I wish for more?

No. I don't want to survive.

I want to *live*.

But this is not just my life. This *is* life and I have to tell you all about it – for me, for everyone. To make sense of things, to understand and to be understood.

Sitting here, looking over the remains of my city and my home, the memories hang heavy around me, filling the air, stifling, and as I breathe them in, they burn my throat and chest like summer heat.

I can't breathe, yet I can remember.

I remember the beginning of 2003. I remember the silent trepidation it brought. What did it mean, that year? To me, it meant more than three years of Mama missing and the frustration of still being no closer to knowing what happened to her. It meant finally telling Papa I didn't want to be a lawyer as Mama had been. It meant exams and university applications.

And it meant war.

To all of us, it meant war. Just a question of when, how and who would survive. Nobody mentioned it on the streets, in the markets, or at school. Of course they didn't. They knew better than that. And so did I. Did anyone even think about who would win? Was I the only one who dared to assume Iraq would fall? That our country would be occupied? Just that thought, that thought in my head, without the words even forming, without my lips opening to speak or to whisper, made me worry, made that fear grow inside me.

I was scared.

And as I sat in the kitchen alone one day listening to the noises of the neighbourhood outside, my friend Layla's younger brothers playing in the street, the market not far away, car horns and chatter, moped engines and the muezzin's call to prayer, I wondered what would change.

What would my city, my home, be like when war came? What would happen? What would be destroyed?

But the possibility of the regime changing, of it falling, seemed unthinkable, unfathomable. I knew what democracy should be, but I couldn't imagine how we would live it, how things would change, how life would be with freedom thrust upon us.

I wanted war to mean we could think freely, speak freely, offer opinion.

I wanted war to mean choice would come.

I wanted war to mean Mama would return home again.

I heard Papa talking to her sometimes, though he never would admit it to me, or to Uncle Aziz, and definitely not to Auntie Hana. He'd tell Mama about his work, the paper he was writing, his students. He'd whisper about the Ba'ath party, sharing with her why he joined, why he had no choice. "It was for protection," he'd say. "To protect my job and our daughter. A member in name only. I do nothing for them," he'd whisper. "*Nothing*."

He'd tell her how her sister Hana was doing, how grumpy she'd become and what a nuisance her children were. He'd tell her about me and I would hear the pauses in his speech, waiting for her reply yet knowing it would never come.

Why? I wondered. *Why do this to yourself?* The one time he talked to me about her, in the days when I still dared to ask, he insisted she was still alive. Countless times I'd seen him emptying out her jewellery box, and I knew he was looking for her necklace, that necklace with the green stone and filigreed gold, but even I knew he would never find it, because she always wore it and would've been wearing it, I'm sure, on that day she disappeared.

That necklace, wherever it was, was wherever Mama was.

When she'd been gone a year I walked into their bedroom and found him standing in front of her open wardrobe, his face pressed against her clothes, his hands holding them to his cheeks and nose and mouth. I moved around to see what he was doing and listened to his heavy breathing as he sucked in the last of her scent before it faded completely from the fabric. He turned and saw me, and for the first time in my life I saw tears in my papa's eyes and stuttering down his face. When I stepped forward to hold him, he growled at me to go.

After that she became a taboo subject in his presence.

Her clothes still hang in the wardrobe.

Or did. Until the bomb.

✤

I opened a new sketchbook, pressing down the white pages, smoothing my fingers along the inside of the spine. I picked up a pencil and held it over the paper, the tip trembling in my fingers. I wanted to make a record of this war, if it arrived. I wanted to remember how things were, what things looked like, draw the buildings in my city that had inspired my dream to be an architect.

Yet I wished I could put my thoughts on paper too, take my worries out of my head, stop them spinning and bouncing around and making me feel sick. Maybe then, I thought, I could sleep at night and my chest wouldn't burn during the day, and I wouldn't feel dizzy at the prospect of bombs and troops, and my head wouldn't hurt with the worry of what might happen.

And I knew the door behind me was locked, but I felt the danger still, faceless, invisible, knowing every secret I held in my head. A lifetime, seventeen years, of being allowed no opinion but the right one, had left me with a fear of expression and a caution to my own thoughts. Could I really write them down? What if it was found? What would happen to me? To Papa? Nobody would know and nobody would ever find out, because we would disappear and nobody would dare to ask where, why or how.

I picked up the sketchbook and stepped from the house. The sun was bright on my eyes and the wind blew around my clothes. *I'll sketch the buildings while they stand,* I thought, *the people while they breathe, and the city while it lives.*

And I wandered around alone, stopping here and there, sketching things that caught my eye, things I wanted to capture while they still existed. I stopped at a market, breathing in the different smells; the fruit, the spices, the tobacco the men smoked, and I sketched the face of a young boy helping his mama, catching a look of cheekiness behind his tight-lipped grin.

I paused to watch a coppersmith, a skinny man with glasses, wipe sweat from his balding head before continuing to beat away at a huge copper pot.

At a row of shops my pencil dashed across the paper; the shapes of the bold signs, the darkened windows, the arches above.

But everywhere I went I saw him. Posters of him, paintings; holding guns, smiling at his people, surrounded by tanks, waving to crowds. Saddam. His presence loomed over us; his mirrored sunglasses hiding his eyes, yet reflecting ours, and our fear. Everywhere I went, I felt him watching.

I found myself at Al-Mustansiriya University, sketching the straight lines of the roof, the patterns on its beige walls, the blackness inside its massive arches. I remembered Papa talking about it, how old it was.

How many people have walked through its doors, I wondered, *in all these hundreds of years it's been standing? How many more will in the future? Will I? Could I?* And

I thought of all the people who were students here, or lecturers, or staff, and all the other people in this city; every one a husband, wife, son, daughter, brother, sister, friend, colleague, teacher, pupil, of someone, somewhere.

Every one, loved by some one.

And I realised that every person in the city would be thinking the same thing, would be wishing, hoping, praying that they wouldn't lose anyone they loved, or they cared for, or even just knew.

But how many would? How many people would be crying in the morning? How much grief would it take, to fill this place of five million people?

I strolled towards home, but there were too many thoughts and worries in my head. I didn't want to be inside. I didn't want to be alone.

I headed towards the river, a place where I knew some friends would be, and together we lounged on the bank, hiding in the shade; everyone solemn. Some had left the country already; those whose families could afford it, or those with relatives abroad, and already it felt like there were holes in our group. Friends missing who would probably never return, yet alive at least. I hoped.

These were friends I'd known for years; friends, it seemed, I'd never not known, and for a moment I watched their faces and a fear hit me that we might never be together again.

With a sigh I turned towards the river and took out my sketchbook. On a clean page the river took shape, flowing away in the distance; grey, concrete bridges spanning it; hotels and high rises reaching up into the pale sky; clumped grasses sprouting near its banks; palm trees, walkways, streets bustling with traffic. Flat and dusty. Sun bleached and muted.

I stopped drawing and stared into the distance, imagining the palace, just visible, watching us. I glanced away from it, in case it caught me staring, in case it read the thoughts that shouldn't have been in my head. I daren't draw it, daren't even look at it. Could only just dare to think about it.

I'd heard whispers about its swimming pools. I closed my eyes and felt the heat envelop me.

If that palace is ever empty, I dared to think, *I will walk along its marble floors in heeled shoes, the noise bouncing off the walls and announcing my presence. I will stroll outside to the swimming pool, slip off my shoes and dive into the cool water. I will swim to the centre and float on my back staring up at the sky, the bluest sky in the world. And I will listen to the silence.*

I opened my eyes and my mouth to share this thought,

but couldn't say the words. Not even to my best friend Layla.

The words weren't even stuck in my throat. They daren't get that far. They daren't even form.

CHAPTER TWO

It was February and the minutes and hours and days and weeks forced us ever closer to the inevitability of which no one spoke.

I was scared. I thought we all were, silently, and I buried myself in my studies, determined to do well, filling my head with facts and figures, hoping to leave no space for worries, hoping to tire my thoughts enough for sleep at night.

I clung to normality and routine, points of reference that held my life together; going to school, seeing friends, strolling around the markets, peering in shop windows.

And as I walked home from school with Layla one day, we talked of our plans for the future; which university to apply to, which course, without admitting to ourselves that these dreams of ours may come to nothing, may turn to dust in front of our eyes.

We spoke of careers we aspired to, and achievements we dreamed of – mine to become an architect, hers to be a teacher – and when we reached our homes, we waved and smiled to each other and went our separate ways. And as I dropped my bag in the doorway and strolled through to the kitchen for food, I found Uncle Aziz and our neighbour Ali, Layla's father, standing in the kitchen with Papa, serious looks on their faces and spades in their hands, an old map spread across the table, held down at its edges by cups or glasses.

I looked to Aziz and he winked at me. I still see it now, that look, frozen in time in my memory, and I feel that warmth it gave me. He could always make me smile; a rotund man with a laugh to match and a bald head that reflected the sun so much I'm sure he must've polished it. He was younger than Papa, although he looked older, with the fuzz around his face making up for the lack of hair on his head. And when he smiled his face would split in two and his eyes would dance with the mischief you would see in boys daring each other to steal fruit from the market place.

He beamed at me, his piano-key teeth still stained with the tobacco he gave up two years ago. 'Lina!' He grabbed me and hugged me, the air squeezing from my lungs. 'Look at you. You've grown so tall and thin.'

I rolled my eyes. 'Uncle Aziz, I saw you two days ago.'

'Yes, my dear, yes. But you're looking thinner. You must be working too hard, studying too hard. You need exercise, fresh air, to build your muscles up. Come.'

What I should've done at the sight of those spades was retreat to my room, with stories of homework and exams, but I'd been caught now, and escape was unlikely. And I liked playing along with Aziz. He made me feel younger, feel a child again. He led me to the back garden, Papa a few paces behind, an unaccustomed smile tickling his face.

'We start here.' Uncle Aziz stuck the spade into the ground and stood firm with his hands on his over-sized hips. 'Dig.'

I picked up the spade and jabbed it at the ground, barely a dent made. 'What are we looking for, Uncle?'

'Water.' He smiled.

I glanced to Papa leaning against the wall, his smile disappearing, Ali standing next to him. My spade hit the ground again, and as I teetered on the blade, I looked to Aziz. 'Somebody bigger would be better at this,' I dared to joke.

His face parted at the mouth, his eyes creasing. He boomed a laugh, and flicked me off the spade like a troublesome fly.

'Yes, your old Uncle has more muscles.' He winked at me again as I picked myself up off the ground.

For the next hour, I watched and fetched and carried. Bringing water and food, or towels to mop brows, as they dug holes across the garden. Though they'd failed to find water, they'd succeeded in making an anti-burglar device – should anyone try to sneak in to the house through the back garden at night, they'd have broken an ankle before making it to the door. Papa, Aziz and Ali dropped the spades to the ground; defeat finally admitted. I inspected the holes. At first I was surprised by the black treacle reaching up and choking the ground, then I understood.

In how many places on this earth would you be disappointed to find oil in your garden?

This dig for water, it turned out, was one of Papa's preparations for war. A colleague of his at the university had a map of old water wells in the city, one of which, it appeared, was directly below our garden. Only it didn't appear. Next, they told me, they'd try Ali's garden, in case the map was inaccurate. I thought to warn Layla of the work that lay ahead of her.

Papa and I did many preparations for war together in the weeks that followed. While taping up windows we didn't say a word to each other, but I was fuming at being kept off school to do something so tiresome. By the time we'd finished there was so much tape on them you could barely see out, and the inside of the house was nearly as dark as the basement beneath us.

He said nothing about why we were doing these things, just "you're staying at home today to help me". But I wanted to go to school. I wanted to see Layla, and Raneen, and Zenab and my other friends. I wanted to chat with them, gossip, have fun, go for a walk after school. I wanted to see if Aliya had managed to talk her mother into getting her the shoes she wanted, if Anita had failed the maths test, if our teacher had had her baby yet.

And I wanted to study.

I didn't want to dig holes, tape windows or cart food supplies into the basement. I didn't want to stand for hours at the gas station filling cans with fuel for when we ran out. I didn't want to go round market stalls with Papa, tripping over sandbags piled next to shop doorways, selling old things to raise enough money to buy a generator.

Always Papa would stop at second-hand shops, though, or at market stalls selling jewellery, and I saw his eyes scan over the necklaces for sale. Someone's once cherished possessions sold for cash to survive the war. I wondered, at first, what he was looking for, but soon I realised.

And I knew what it meant to him that it wasn't there – that it must still be with her, somewhere, that green necklace with the filigreed gold.

I could do nothing to help him, and, selfishly, I wanted to get on with my life.

Why so much food? I wanted to ask. *Why do we need bottles of water? Why a generator?* But my papa was not one for conversation or for answers.

I was desperate to know what would happen when the war began. There was no 'if' any more, every sunrise bringing more inevitability. I didn't follow the news as I suppose I should've, and people didn't say much, but I watched the streets and the people and I felt the mood. Fear on people's faces was the easiest emotion to read, and the news gave no answers, even if you dared to think the questions. I wanted to know, was desperate to know, what would happen and how long for. What about school? My hopes for university? What about my friends? What about Mama? What would it be like after?

What would be left?

Who would be left?

Would I?

CHAPTER THREE

On that day in March, which so many of us will never forget, Papa and I closed the windows, locked the doors, turned off the lights and – with a last look around – headed into the basement.

We sat on a mattress together, leaning up against the wall, surrounded by boxes and cartons, bottles of water and food, all sorts of everything. Papa looked at me with his arms outstretched and I curled myself into his embrace and waited for the bombs to come.

At the top of one of the walls was a tiny window, barely large enough to be of any use for anything, but while we waited, our eyes never left it. What we were waiting for, I'm not sure, and as the minutes ticked on, I wondered if it would happen at all. Were all the preparations for nothing? All the anticipation and dread and worry?

I felt it before I heard it. A rumble. A plane approaching? The window rattled. The ground shook under me, grumbling, then a bang.

No, not a bang – an *explosion*, a torrent of sound. Then another, the noise tearing through the air, ripples and echoes following it. I felt my body tense, leaned in to Papa. He stroked my hair, his breath even on my face.

And the window lit up orange.

And the basement rocked.

And the world was torn to pieces around us.

I squeezed closer to Papa and I felt his breath quicken, his heart race. I looked to his face and saw what I didn't want to see. I saw fear in his dark eyes. He rocked me back and forth, watching the window. And I glanced up to it, and in a second it filled with white.

Time paused.

Silence.

Then I blinked. A green blur flashed in front of my eyes in the darkness. Papa threw me to the ground, covered me with his body.

The ground shook, my home shook. The window blew out and the sound and the force hit us with a punch. I felt it with every part of my body. My lungs expelling air, my heart trying to beat out of my chest, the thudding echoing in my ears. My legs weak, my hands clenching, my nails digging crescents into my skin. Fear coursed through me and sweat dripped from me as I waited for the next and the next and the next. I waited for the death which I was sure was searching for me.

I think I screamed. I think I cried. I was a baby in my papa's arms and I wanted him to protect me. To save me. To keep me from harm. I closed my eyes and wished I could block out the sound. But it continued. Torrential, consuming, raucous noise. I tried to pick out sounds: alarms rhythmic, blaring; the roar of explosions; aircraft tearing through the skies; gunfire too loud to be gunfire; constant thunder.

Then calm, and we would breathe. We would catch each other's eye. Was it over? Was that it? Had we survived?

And it would start again.

Shattering of glass, cracking of walls, the shaking of our doors upstairs, chairs crashing over above us. My mind, my imagination, went wild. What was happening outside? What had been hit? What was on fire? What would be left? What about my school? I saw pictures, images in my head. I saw my classroom, my books scattered around the floor, the wall missing, concrete and rubble in piles, desks destroyed, fire approaching, burning, eating its way through the corridors, edging towards my work, then engulfing it, consuming it.

My head showed me my worst fears. I felt helpless. I saw Mama in prison, the walls caving in around her, burying her; the guards running out, laughing, leaving her. I saw Aziz in his taxi, desperate to drive his fare home before the bombs began, and the road disappearing in an explosion in front of him, the plume of smoke rising into the sky, eating its way through the air. I saw Layla in a hospital bed, bandages over her face, blood seeping through, her parents not at her bedside, alone. I rubbed my eyes, shook my head, desperate to keep my imagination under control, to stop my feelings of dread.

And then the morning would come, and with it, would come quietness.

✣

Night after night, far too many nights for me to remember, or want to remember, the bombing continued. And with every bang, every crash, every explosion, I waited, expecting our house to be hit. For my world to end. I couldn't think about tomorrow, that maybe next it was my turn to die.

And after a while, I no longer cried. But my body still shook, fearing for my life, for Papa's life, for Auntie Hana and Aziz and their horrid children, for Layla and her family, for all my friends, for my teachers, for the shopkeepers and the market traders. For Mama.

Our small window, fixed again, gave us clues. We prayed not to see fire, we prayed for no explosions so close to us that we could see orange or yellow or white. We prayed for no rubble. And in the morning, waking us from the little sleep we may have had, dusty sunlight would filter through and we would stare at each other for a moment, run our hands gently on each other's faces, checking we weren't dreaming, amazed and thankful that we, at least, had made it through another night. And with dread weighing us down like lead, we would open the door to our house and prepare ourselves for what we would find.

With all the bombs, and noises, and explosions and ground-shaking, it seemed impossible that anything could still have been alive out there. Time after time, I stepped out from the basement thinking Papa and I would be the only ones left. Alone in a deserted, bombed-out, destroyed city.

It became almost habit. We would check our house

for damage; we would check the water supply, the electricity, the doors and windows. The first night we lost our water, the second night, the electricity. Then we would open the door and step outside into the scars and damage the city had to show us. I would look over to Layla's house to make sure it was still there.

One morning, after a terrible night of bombing, we left straight away to visit Uncle Aziz and Aunt Hana, desperate to know what had become of them.

The day began well: we were not dead, and Layla's house was still standing. These things gave us hope.

We lived close to the centre of the city, where there were many targets for the Americans. And so on the way to check on Aziz and Hana, the hope we held high in our chests was eaten away as we saw horror upon horror.

Unbearable suffering; sights you didn't want to look at, but couldn't peel your eyes away from. So much pain: quiet tears with angry faces. I felt guilty for being alive and unhurt. I felt constantly in shock, forever on the verge of tears that could help no one. We put our heads down and we walked, and when we arrived at Aziz's house and saw it still standing, relief flooded our faces with tears.

We stayed awhile, with little to talk about but war

and its effects; shops that were closed, schools that were bombed, neighbours or friends who had died.

"Will I still be able to go to university?" I asked Papa.

Hana interrupted, tutting and shaking her head. "Don't fill the girl's head with nonsense," she said.

I knew Papa disagreed with her, I knew he wanted me to study, but he didn't reply to her, didn't argue or attempt discussion.

And soon after, we headed home again.

❖

Our relationship changed as we sat together in that basement waiting for bombs. We talked. About war, about democracy, about what might happen to a country suddenly liberated. Papa told me he didn't believe it would be over quickly. He spoke of people with aspirations of power and leadership, all vying for a place; of corruption and capitalism and oil and Vietnam and Russia and civil war.

And along the way, I asked him questions, and I felt we were becoming more than father and daughter. Somehow, we were becoming friends.

Once, when he had finished talking, and that awkward silence again filled the basement as we waited for the roar of the planes and the bombs, he took me over to where the stairs met the wall. He dragged a chair across and told me to stand on it, told me to pull away the broken bricks, put my hand down the gap in the wall. I pulled out a metal box.

"It's for you," he sighed. "If I'm not here. If anything goes wrong. If Mama doesn't come back. There's fifteen thousand dollars. I saved it. In case there was a ransom for your Mama, but…" He shrugged. "If that never comes… If things are too bad, then you must leave, study somewhere else, somewhere safe."

I put my hand out to him, but he drew away.

"Baghdad is a wonderful city, it used to be one of the finest places to study, with the best universities, but it won't be safe for a long time and if I'm not here to look after you…"

He didn't finish his sentence.

I asked him why we couldn't both go now, why we couldn't start a new life together, but he just looked at me and told me he could never leave her; that without her, there was no new life, there was no life.

Three and a half years, and still he believed she would come back. And while he believed, so did I, because I could never break his heart.

CHAPTER FOUR

Sometimes the bombs were so loud, and the ground shook so much, I imagined the earth was splitting, a crack forming, chasing its way to me and Papa, stretching wider and wider as it sneaked towards us without us knowing. I imagined that with the next explosion it would reach us, the basement floor would open up and the earth would eat us alive.

One of those nights, still sleeping in the basement, I dreamed our house was hit and it crashed down upon us. We were captured in the basement, encased in a concrete prison, trapped by the rubble of our own life. And we waited for rescue, but no one came. Then when freedom came to the city, Mama returned, and she dug us out with her bare hands, split and bleeding. But when she found us, we had died. And she cried and cried; cursing herself, saying that if she had come home a minute earlier or walked faster, we would still be alive.

I told Papa about that dream and he looked at me with such compassion and love that I finally found the courage to ask him what had happened to Mama.

I knew she had disappeared, of course. I was aware that one day she was there and the next she was not, and that afterwards Papa would not again speak the name of Saddam. And I thought she had been taken, but I had never asked about the details. I had never wanted to *know* the details, because knowing them might make her gone forever.

Papa rubbed his eyes, ran his fingers through his curly hair, and through the banging and crashing of bombs, and the ground shaking and the house foundations moaning, he finally told me.

"On October 28th 1999, at half past four, I went into a meeting at work. As I left my desk, my phone rang. I ignored it; I didn't want to be late. Five minutes later, as I sat in the room, talking to my bosses, my mobile rang. I apologised, and turned it off without checking who was calling. Ten minutes later the secretary knocked on the door and told me I had a visitor. I was annoyed. My boss was looking to see if I was suitable for promotion. I asked the secretary to tell the visitor to call back tomorrow.

"A few minutes later, there was shouting coming from the corridor and doors opening and banging shut, and Tariq, a man who worked with your Mama, barged into the office shouting and waving his arms around. To me it was a stream of words; I couldn't tell what he was talking about. It was my boss who understood what had happened.

"Your Mama had been arrested. She… she had just gone and I… I'd been too wrapped up in what I was doing to think. What if I'd answered the phone in my office, or my mobile? I could've followed. I could've found her. Got her back again."

His voice trailed away and I kept my eyes away from him, afraid that if he looked at me he would've seen my face saying he was a fool to think that. Probably I would have neither of them now.

"Your Mama's legal success rate had earned her respect from unlikely admirers. She was wanted by the… the highest authority, to serve them. That went against everything she believed. Refusing the offer to work for them was to defy the regime and its leader. That wasn't acceptable. She refused to bow to pressure.

"I can guess where they took her. I reported her

missing, of course, but after a week of going to the police every day I was told it would be in my, and your, best interests if I didn't return. That I should forget her and if I did keep coming back, you might not have a papa any more. I couldn't put you in danger. Your mama had purposefully kept going to work, not hidden away from them, or run away, to keep them from us."

I had listened to whispered gossip on street corners and knew some of what happened to those who were arrested, especially those considered to be political prisoners. I had heard the stories of torture. But I never knew if it was true or not, and there was nobody to ask. Were they urban myths made to keep us in fear? Or true accounts from the few who made it out alive? I didn't know. I assumed Papa had heard these things too. I wondered how he managed to keep his hope in her still being alive. What would he have left if he could no longer hope for her return?

As I sat in the protection of his arms listening to the bombs drop, I thought of the possibilities: if Mama was still in prison, had been there for nearly three and a half years, then how much suffering had she endured? Was she still enduring? Was it selfish of Papa and me to want her to still be alive, if every day for her brought more torture? Was it better to believe she was dead, and had been released from her pain?

But *I* wanted her to be alive.

I wanted there to be a knock at the door and when I opened it, for Mama to be standing in front of me with a smile on her face, the sun reflecting off her black hair, her green eyes glinting with love.

I wanted her to pick me up off my feet and hold me tight, the smell of her wrapping round me, her warm breath on my skin, her eyelashes fluttering like butterflies on my cheek.

And I wanted time to stop at that moment, and never start again.

Papa said very little for the rest of the night and when I woke in the morning I was lying on the mattress pressed into the corner of the basement, a steaming cup of tea left on the floor for me.

As I walked around the house that day, thoughts of Mama rushed around my head, and for the first time in a very long time I saw the shadow of her memory; fleeting, hiding in the edge of my vision. She breezed through the door after a day at work. She stood at the cooker, turning her head to smile at me, and strolled towards me while I sat at the table. I closed my eyes and felt her presence. I kept my eyes closed because I knew that when I opened them, she wouldn't be there. Would she ever be there?

❖

I felt desperate to get out of the house, so I closed the door behind me, leaving those memories of Mama inside, and I called for Layla. Together we walked down to the river, barely a word shared between us, because the only words that came to my head were those of war and sadness.

And as we walked I hoped that my friends would be there, that they were alive, as I always assumed they would be, as I used to assume Mama would be. It went without saying. Just as you assume your house will still be standing when you wake in the morning, the windows and the doors, the rugs and the curtains, were all there when I went to bed, as was Papa that day and my friends. Why shouldn't they be there in the morning?

Change was hanging over my city like a black cloud. I wanted to tell Layla about Mama, but the words weren't there. I wanted to ask her about her family, but was scared to hear the answers. Instead we walked in silence, words not necessary, our friendship holding us together.

CHAPTER FIVE

Everything became so wretched. Bad news came every day and to everyone. Good news was if you awoke in the morning, and if you survived the day. We lived as animals, thinking only of survival.

How did I feel? Like I was living on a knife edge. Like there wasn't enough air to fill my lungs. Like I should be grateful for being alive. Like I should be making the most of my life because it could so easily be taken away. But there was no way to do this. I was scared. So scared.

Papa's friend was killed and I cried although I barely knew him. He was running home, through a residential area, and a bomb landed. Not on him. Not close enough for him to be lifted off his feet with the force of the blast. But close enough for a piece of shrapnel to hit him in the stomach.

He died in a hospital bed among hundreds of others, all waiting for a doctor or a nurse. He died with a six-year-old boy on one side of him, half a leg missing, his face and arms covered in dirt and blood.

Rumours flew around like grains of sand. Americans killing civilians and children because they were in the way; Iraqis targeting their own, bombing their own civilians, yet blaming the Americans.

Two of my friends' houses were destroyed. They survived but were forced to live with relatives, their brothers and sisters sent in different directions, families divided. Those who left the country, I don't know what happened to them, I wish I did.

❖

Then Baghdad fell.

My city, my home, was occupied. Americans were everywhere. Tanks. Guns. Soldiers.

It scared me. I didn't know how to feel or what to do. My life was on hold. I wanted to go to school, but couldn't, and worry filled what space was left in my head. What about my exams? My application to university? But there was nothing I could do about it. Everyone I met, everyone I talked to, had a million questions, but nobody had any answers.

The Americans shouted their orders in their brusque English, but so many didn't understand them. I'm lucky my English is good, I have Papa to thank for that, speaking English around the house, keen for me to learn early and learn properly. His fluency and his vocabulary hadn't come from Western films and music like so many people's had; it came from living and studying there for years.

"English history books teach you a different kind of English," he told me.

When I hear the Americans talk, I think they could do with some lessons from Papa.

Was I glad the regime had fallen? Yes, I suppose, I was. But so frightened and so worried.

Papa and Aziz talked about it over dinner – they chatted and argued and debated about what it would mean to us as a country and as a people. Papa, always the historian, reasoned his argument with fact, Aziz went with what he saw and what he felt. As I watched them and listened to them I sensed the change already; they were Iraqis and they were talking. But even when the debate heated up, it ended in one of two ways: either Aziz's contagious laugh forcing up the corners of Papa's mouth, or Hana mentioning the prisons, questioning when they would be opened, and the prisoners liberated. The opposite ends of the scale, one lightening your heart, the other making it feel like lead. Both bringing the family together.

I saw clouds cross Papa's eyes whenever prison was mentioned. I saw the muscles fall slightly in his face.

Life in the city was beyond dangerous, a curfew in the evening, gunfire across the skies, explosions rattling the windows and doors in their frames. I felt closer to Papa than I ever had. We were a strange family for this city, this country. I didn't know of any other single fathers and I thought of what he did, bringing me up alone, waiting for Mama's return, and I wondered if he was lonely. He went to work and came home. He did very little else. And I wondered if his belief in Mama's eventual return ever dwindled, if he ever dared to let himself think she wouldn't come back.

Maybe if he had, he would've taken Aziz's advice; left this country, returned to England, found a job there, at least until Baghdad was safe. Things would have been better if he had done so, if he had left. Things would not have ended as they did.

But his belief in her survival seemed forever undaunted, and he stayed.

Some days I believed she wasn't meant to be found, that I should accept she would never come back. Other days I believed it was kinder to think she had died. I knew there had been no justice in this city, and still it eluded us, but always a smallest shadow of hope, the tiniest chink of belief, lurked somewhere inside me, and I could never let go of the possibility that one day she might just return to us.

But as we waited and we hoped, our lives continued to change before our eyes.

I watched strange men, in strange uniforms and with strange voices, march and drive into my city with weapons at their shoulders, pointing right, left, up, down, uttering promises of a better life. Safety and security. Freedom and democracy. Liberation.

When these things would come, I never heard.

I saw shops with fronts blasted out, schools with roofs caving in, holes in roads, burnt-out cars, piles of rubble that had been homes, plumes of smoke, shells of buildings, husbands comforting crying wives, mothers nursing injured children.

People at school disappeared; stopped coming, were

injured, some killed. My class was suddenly only twelve.

I cried. Selfishly, I cried for everything I had lost. I missed my friends so much. I sat next to different students, spent my lunch times and breaks with girls I had never spoken to before. I felt lonely. I hoped it might bring a sense of camaraderie between us; all in the same position, all with the same feelings, but it didn't. It brought a bigger division.

One of the girls asked me what it was like being the only Christian in the class. I was shocked. She said she couldn't sit with me. "Baghdad isn't a place for Christians," she told me. "You should leave."

Teachers left too. My science teacher, my favourite teacher, was forced to leave. A member of the Ba'ath party, he had no choice. But he was ambitious, hopeful and aspiring for his future; he joined, I'm sure, in name only, like Papa. To achieve anything, to get anywhere, to be promoted, to thrive in your career, was impossible if you didn't join.

But to the Americans, you were a Ba'athist, so you were a threat – your job was taken.

And so Papa lost his job too. His passion for education and learning which had followed him throughout his life, pulled from under him. I could see the disappointment in his shoulders, the depression tugging at his body and his mind, the frustration in his eyes at being unable to help his students, who battled in to the university, past roadblocks and checkpoints, through explosions and gunfire. His students so loyal to him.

My poor Papa. He was lost. He was drifting.

I wished I could do something for him. Help him in some way, but there was nothing I, nor anyone else, could do.

And now, what do I wish for?

I wish that I had thought of something, anything, before it was too late.

CHAPTER SIX

With time on his hands, and with danger everywhere, Papa insisted on walking me and Layla to school, taking turns with Ali.

Before the war, I used to love the walk to school, even on days when I had an exam. Strolling by with Layla and her brothers, the sounds of a city coming to life, the smells from the bakeries, the morning sun prickling out sweat on our brows as we gossiped about fellow students, moaned about homework or bad grades or miserable teachers. I didn't have to be taken to school every day in fear of kidnapping, attacks or rape.

Now, as we walked with Papa, we dodged through rubbish piling up on streets, counted bullet holes in abandoned cars; Layla's brothers jumped over charred marks on the pavements where something had exploded or been set on fire.

And as it soon came to be that females daren't go outside without a male escort, so it came to be that we could no longer dress as we liked.

This was our liberation.

I called for Layla one morning, and felt the change at my shoulder. It followed me, shadowing, eating and destroying, threatening everything I held precious. I looked at Layla and barely recognised her.

She always wore jeans, she always wore her dark hair pinned a certain way, but now? I looked at her, a long abaya covering her body, a hijab covering her head. "*Why?*" I whispered.

"My mother is worried," she told me. "She doesn't even want me to go to school. Not even with an escort. This is the only way she'll let me out of the house. She says it's safer."

I thought about her answer, staring around as we walked. I saw the girls, the women. Not one female without a male escort, most with two, all with their heads covered, some wearing abayas, covered to their feet.

How long has it been like this? I asked myself. *Have I*

*been walking around with my eyes closed? Why have I not
noticed?*

I turned back to Layla.

"Think about it, Lina," she said.

Think about it, I repeated in my head. If I'd said it
aloud, the incredulity would've been so heavy I wouldn't
have been able to take another step. I didn't want to be
told what I could and couldn't wear. I didn't want to
wear a hijab, I wanted to feel the breeze blowing at my
long hair.

At school that day, I was the only female with her
head uncovered. Whatever the religion, the upbringing,
the faith, the girls were united by a hijab. At lunch I sat
behind a group of girls who were debating something
in hushed whispers. Briefly Layla leaned towards me.
"They're talking about Anita. She was kidnapped
yesterday. If her family don't pay the ransom by tonight,
she'll be killed."

Anita had been my partner in maths class for a year.
She had lived down our street when she was younger.
She had a large family, three brothers, a sister and a
multitude of aunts and uncles. Her mother had asked her
and her brother to go to the market. Only the brother
came back.

I felt sick. What was happening to us?

It was unbelievable. And there were more and more stories like that. Where was the freedom and democracy we were promised? This wasn't freedom. Not being able to walk to school, to go to the market, to have a head uncovered, to be proud to be Christian. Layla, my best friend, who I'd shared everything with for so many years, was scared to sit next to me in class or at dinner, because I was a Christian, and went with my head uncovered.

I felt anger and frustration grow in me. My head ached with it. I wanted to scream and cry. Stamp my feet like a two-year-old until somebody promised it would all stop.

When Ali came to talk to Papa the next day, I listened at the doorway. He said we could no longer walk to school together, they could no longer be seen associating with us, us Christians, he couldn't risk them being persecuted.

Persecuted by who? I wondered. Not the Americans. By our fellow Iraqis? Extremists? Fundamentalists? I didn't know where these people had come from – it was as if they had been locked away somewhere, and when the Americans came, they brought the key to let them out.

Something else had been taken from me. Something

so simple: a walk to school with a friend. There were no words in my head to argue. There was no explanation.

Before the war most people knew little of who was what religion; Sunnis would marry Shia and live alongside Christians. I didn't understand why it had changed but I knew Christians were not wanted nor welcome in the city; they were attacked, homes ransacked, death threats given. Employers told them to leave, afraid of what might happen if they were seen to be friends with one. We lost friends, smiling neighbours and respect. And it seemed I had lost Layla.

But I did understand her father's fears.

A few days later, while I was out with Papa, and wearing a pair of trousers and a shirt, my hair blowing around, we stopped at a second-hand shop. I don't remember the excuse he gave, but I knew what he was looking for as he peered through the dusty glass.

I heard someone shout behind me and I turned. A face running towards me, something in his hands. I frowned, confused as to what was happening, not understanding who he was shouting at, who he was running for. But it was me. And suddenly I was on the floor, trying to figure out what had happened.

I felt the wetness seeping through my shirt, felt it

clinging and burning at my skin, the pain eating at me as Papa dragged me through the streets. And as Papa pulled me back home, ordered me into the bathroom, I realised acid had been thrown over me. Why? Because of how I was dressed? Because I'm Christian? I didn't know. A warning maybe? I was lucky – only my scalp was burned, my arm blistered. My face had not been touched – I had turned in time. And Papa removed my shirt in time. But I trembled as I stood in the bath, pouring water down my front over and over again; I could still see his face, that look in his eyes.

When I re-emerged, Papa handed me a long skirt and a hijab. And I didn't argue.

CHAPTER SEVEN

Within a couple of weeks, Papa had a new job.

When he told me what he'd be doing I felt sick to my stomach, my hands shaking in my lap, my head spinning. The shock of it, even though so much time has passed, still burns through my veins.

Papa stepped into the house with a stack of papers in his hands, put them away from my view and asked me to sit down.

He sighed. "I'm going to be interpreting for the Americans," he said, "for the troops."

In silence I stared at him, waiting, hoping for him to tell me it was a joke.

"Sometimes I'll travel around with them, sometimes I'll be with them when houses are raided, sometimes when people are questioned."

My head was filled with such disbelief I couldn't find the words to reply. Unbelievable wasn't the word. Unthinkable, perhaps. I didn't understand his decision. I didn't understand why he would want to work for them. The air was thick with rumours of what the troops were doing to civilians. Why did Papa want to be a part of that?

I hoped they were just rumours, that there was no truth in them. But still, the danger he was putting himself in was... was... what? Appalling? Unbelievable? No, they are just words, and words didn't do justice to what I was feeling inside. I was scared for him. And for myself. I didn't want him to be hurt. I didn't want him to see the things I had heard of. He shouldn't be in situations where he would see death and suffering and pain. But then... wasn't that what everyone in this country was seeing?

But I wanted to keep my papa safe. I wanted him home with me every evening. I wanted to cling to him and not let him out of my sight. Some days the fear in me was so great, the worry that I would come home and he wouldn't be there any more, that I wanted to stay out, put off going home, unwilling to face what might have happened.

"It's a good job, Lina, pays well, and we need the money," he said.

I tried to keep the tears from my eyes, and stop them stinging my cheeks.

"I'll see a lot of Baghdad. Probably visit the police stations and the prisons. See... see the people inside."

And at that, there was nothing left for me to say.

Though I understood, I shook my head at him and left the room.

✥

For Papa's first few weeks of his new job, he would recount his day to me over the dinner table. He started off telling me how well he got on with the soldiers. Some had shown him photos of loved ones back home, and he had shared with one of them what had happened to Mama. He told me many were just young boys, scared of the situation they were in, jittery when nervous, a little trigger happy; desperate to prove their worth to their colleagues and superiors. Sometimes he came home with things they'd given him. Some cigarettes he could sell, some chocolate he'd give to me.

Perhaps I've been worrying too much, I thought. *Perhaps this job will be fine for him.*

But gradually he spoke less and less. His shoulders drooped lower and lower, and his face aged, the lines and contours deeper, a little greyer, dustier.

And I would ask him how work was, but he had no answers for me. And I saw blood on his shoes. I heard him crying in his room. I worried about him more than ever. I worried about our future.

CHAPTER EIGHT

I heard the footsteps first. Two sets, I thought, heavy boots across the garden, moving closer.

I saw the shadows next, two shadows passing the kitchen window. Then a knock on the door and I turned and saw uniform through the frosted glass, a soldier's uniform.

I felt sick.

I glanced at the clock in the kitchen – it was too early for Papa.

My heart pounded in my chest, but I didn't move. I held my breath, and I waited. Should I answer? Should I run? Should I get Papa's gun and point the barrel through the window?

I was alone, and there were soldiers outside. And that fear and that worry held me motionless as I watched the door handle ease down, the hinges creak and sunlight stream through the gap.

I couldn't scream, I couldn't shout, I couldn't even move.

I closed my eyes, took a deep breath, tried to swallow away my fear, tried to imagine them gone. Whoever they were.

And when I dared to open my eyes again, I saw Aziz first. Then standing next to him I saw a soldier, an American soldier, and my eyes flicked over his khaki uniform, his dusty boot, his helmet clasped under an arm, his dark glasses dangling from his fingers.

His hands streaked with dirt, his jacket smeared with blood.

Whose blood?

My breathing came thick and fast, my chest burning, my eyes stinging. I glanced up to his face, so far above me, and into his eyes for just a second before he looked away.

I knew, then, but I didn't want to know.

The American soldier ran his fingers through his dirty blonde hair, and I saw his chest heave as he sighed. I didn't want to know why he was there, I didn't want him to speak, didn't want to hear anything that he might have to say to me.

I turned to walk away.

"Lina, please," Aziz whispered, taking my hand in his. "He's come here to talk to you. He wanted to. He asked to."

And with a sigh, knowing I had no choice, I did what Aziz asked of me; I sat at the table and the enemy sat down to face me. Aziz poured coffee for us and as the steam lifted into the air between us, I wished this soldier would disappear into it, along with whatever it was he had to say.

But my wish went unanswered.

I could hear his heavy breathing. I could smell his uniform and his war.

I waited for him to speak, for his mouth to open and the words that I was dreading to come out. The brightness of my fear exploded in front of my eyes and burned inside my chest.

I watched his rough, dusty fingers and his clumsy hands that pulled triggers gently brush the edge of his cup. I watched his eyes flicker from the table, to me, to Aziz, to the door, to the window, resting nowhere.

And at last, but with barely a whisper, the silence was broken. "I worked with Joe, your dad," he said.

No, I thought. *No, no, no.*

I wanted to put my hands over my ears, close my eyes and make it all go away. My chest was red hot, my hands were shaking. I looked to Aziz, sitting next to me, fear and dread and panic shooting through my body, my fingertips burning with it, my cheeks flushing. I wanted his face to split into that familiar smile or his booming laugh to fill the room. I wanted him to tell me not to worry. That everything was fine.

But he said nothing, and he did not laugh. And as the soldier, this stranger in my home, in my country, began talking again, I felt Aziz squeeze my hand and although my ears didn't want me to, I listened to the words, listened to him tell me Papa was dead.

And my tears fell and everything else faded away.

I felt everything yet nothing. Anger and loneliness. Hatred and emptiness. Confusion and heartache and shock and denial. My head was in chaos, but my body was numb.

I stood up. I had to get away. Had to get away from this man, this soldier.

My legs buckled underneath me, my strength gone, and I fell to the ground. And I laid there, for a long time, on the kitchen floor, Aziz next to me, rocking me back and forth. Sobbing.

I wished I was dead.

I wished I'd died before I'd been told about Papa. Before it had happened even. My head didn't want to be filled with those images, and my heart didn't want to think of life without him; it was barely imaginable. Was I now truly an orphan?

The air drained from me as I sobbed, my lungs burning, and although I wanted to die, my body still sucked in breath.

Could they do any more to me? my head screamed. *Could they take any more? What have I done for this to happen?*

And I felt myself lifted up.

Aziz held me to his chest, sat with me on the sofa, and rocked me like the baby I was in his arms. He stroked my hair and dried my tears and when finally I looked up to him, I saw tears running down his face too. I wanted to run out into the street, shout at it, shout at the city and the country and all the people in it. All the people that made up this stupid war. I wanted to shout and scream at the stupid Americans and their lapdogs, the British, the Spanish, the Australians, the Polish, the Danish. There was so much anger pouring down my veins I didn't know what to do with it.

It was like when Mama disappeared. I felt useless and weak and pathetic.

"It was a dangerous job your Papa had, Lina. In a city that's dangerous just to live in." Aziz sighed.

I dragged myself up and I launched myself at the soldier, arms and legs flailing at him, kicking, screaming, punching and scratching at him. In that split second I wanted to kill him. I wanted to tear his tongue out for telling me, tear his eyes out for watching Papa die, for not helping him, tear him apart for just being there. My anger, my blame focused on the soldier, not the person, in front of me.

But he gently, carefully, held me at arm's length while my tirade battered him. He lifted his eyes to mine muttering apology after apology as Aziz tried to pull me away. I felt his hands shaking and I thought I saw tears on his face.

I stopped and hung my head in shame.

"I'm sorry," he whispered again.

I wanted to say I was, but couldn't speak, whatever emotion, whether grief, confusion, hatred, fear or sorrow, held back the words.

I couldn't think, didn't know what to think.

Papa, my papa, was dead?

"I..." began the American soldier. "I... ah... I wanted to tell you about it myself. So you'd know. I wanted you to know... how it happened."

I stared at him.

"Would you like to know?"

I took a deep breath. "Yes."

The soldier looked down at his hands. He didn't look up again, as the words came tumbling out of him, like if he looked at me, he would not be able to continue.

"When Joe arrived this morning, the place was a little different, everyone was busy... some of the soldiers were agitated and nervous, a couple excited. There was like an edge about the place, adrenalin pumping round, y'know? We were being sent to check out the house of some suspected weapons dealer, Joe was to come with us, to interpret, and talk to the guys, keep them calm and stuff. It wasn't a good district we were heading to, and y'know, I'd worked with Joe for a good while, and I knew when he looked nervous. Hell, I was nervous. We gave him a bulletproof vest. It had an American flag on it, on his chest."

He paused, tapping his chest to show where it was. He ran his over-sized fingers through his hair, and scratched the back of his neck.

"He didn't like it. He'd said it before and on the way, in the back of the truck he moaned about it some more. 'I'm not an American,' he said. 'What'll my people think? It's like an advertisement on my chest.'

"I told him to pick it off and one of the other soldiers gave him a pin they had stuck in their uniform. Anyhow, they got chatting. Joe was interested in people, y'know? He liked to hear their stories, where they were from, and that. So he sat chatting with Eric. He was from Texas and spoke with such a drawl, you wanted to put a cowboy hat on his head and ask him where his horse was tethered.

"Eric was in a better mood than anyone else, he was heading home in the morning, told Joe he was hanging near the back, taking it easy and looking after him. I listened to them chat like old buddies, about family back home, Eric's mom and dad, his sister and his little brother, about Joe's wife, your mom, about you. Eric showed him a photo of his little brother playing in the Texan desert with a toy rifle. Wanted to be a soldier just like Eric.

"Anyhow, when we got there, some of them went inside, I stayed out, marking the doorway, Eric went further back with Joe waiting 'til someone was brought out to be questioned. We didn't want to take him in, it was too dangerous.

"There was a load of shouting and banging from inside. I looked back to Eric. He looked worried, he lifted his gun to his shoulder, stopped chewing his gum.

"Soldiers came out dragging a couple of men, their hands behind their heads."

He paused to shake his head and I watched his fingers going round and round the rim of the cup, trembling.

"Two women came chasing out after them, and their voices were, like, so high and shrill. Their arms were flapping around all over the place. Then their neighbours started joining in the noise. You could hear them shouting stuff, but we hadn't a clue what they were saying, and Joe was picking out some of it, telling us they were yelling 'innocent, innocent,' and all sorts of name calling and insults. Soldiers shouted over the lot and it was just a mess, English and Arabic, accents, crying, screaming. Hell, it was just mad.

"And Eric, his gun pointed from one to another, watching for danger. They took the men over to Joe and I saw them look at that flag on his chest, half picked off, flapping as Joe moved. The men were shoved down to their knees in front of him and they babbled through a barrage of questions.

"I saw Joe lift his head to the sky. I'd seen him do that

before, like he was looking for some quiet to think. As I looked round again, I saw a young boy, about ten years old maybe, come running out from the building, a gun, a damn big one, to his shoulder."

The soldier moved his hands away from the cup and his fingers clenched.

"Above everything else, I heard the boy. I heard one word – Papa.

"He pointed his gun at Eric. Next to him, Joe froze. Eric's gun pointed at the boy. His head cocked to one side, his eyes staring down the sights. I pointed my gun at the boy. But, y'know, he was a *boy*, like Eric's little brother, playing at being a soldier.

"Eric moved sideways, away from Joe, and the gun in the boy's hands, a full-sized gun, not a toy, followed him. It was like slow motion and we all seemed to pause forever.

"Then one person shot." He shrugged. "Then everyone did. I fell to the floor, trying to pick out what was happening through all the dust and noise and bodies everywhere, trying not to hit my own men.

"And as quick as it had started, it stopped. And the shouting and screaming stopped and there was this, this kind of stillness. Everything was a mess. I couldn't work out what had happened; who'd shot first, who'd shot who. I didn't dare count the bodies. I looked for my men, and I saw the boy and Eric. Both down. But Joe, he was still standing, he was still alive."

All this time I'd been watching his hands and his fingers, his untouched coffee going cold in front of him. And now I felt him look at me, and I lifted my head and saw his eyes, his bright blue eyes, and now they held mine as he spoke. And I blinked and the tears ran down my cheeks, but still this soldier held my gaze now. And through the blurriness I saw his mouth tremble, I saw him try to swallow his emotion and I saw him blink away what I felt sure were tears.

This soldier.

"Joe stood up. I shouted at him to get down and take cover but he ignored me. He looked to the boy, then to Eric, and back again. Everyone was shouting at him to get down, but he looked torn, like he didn't know which way to go. And I'm shouting at the top of my lungs. But he walked, just walked, really calmly, to Eric.

"I should've run to him, I know I should've. I should've knocked him flat but I just stood there shouting at him to get down."

He paused and took a breath.

"He walked all the way over to Eric, calmly as anything, and knelt down next to him. I started running towards him, saw him put his hand on Eric's chest and look up to the sky. And then…" His voice lowered. "There was a shot. One single shot and he was down… "He died as I reached him," the soldier whispered. "It hit him…" I watched him close his eyes, watched his trembling hand lift and his fingers tap his head. "I held him then. I held him while he died."

I saw the blood on the soldier's jacket again, and I knew then, that it was Papa's blood.

My papa's blood.

CHAPTER NINE

Whatever happened to Sacha? Part I

OCTOBER 1999

Sacha saw the car outside, waiting. Two men standing next to it. She knew who they were, that they had come for her. And she knew that the short walk out of the front doors of the law firm would be the last she would take in freedom for a long time.

In the middle of the foyer her feet paused and she thought for a moment. What could she do? Where could she go? What options did she have?

And she realised she had none.

Her fingers reached up to the necklace resting on her chest, stroking the green stone and the filigreed gold around it. And as she slipped it into her pocket, she stepped forward, across the foyer and out of the front doors. Away not just from the air-conditioning and comfortable office, but from her life and out into the searing heat and stark sunshine, to be taken away to whatever fate waited for her.

The bag went over her head and Baghdad disappeared from her view.

She didn't scream, or shout for help.

She didn't fight, or try to escape.

If they couldn't have her, she knew they would take her family instead.

The handcuffs dug into her wrists. The air under the bag grew hot and moist; no space for her breath to escape, or fresh air to find its way in.

She closed her eyes, concentrating on her breathing, keeping herself calm. She thought of her friend Tariq watching her leave the office, worry marking his forehead. She hoped he would call her husband. She hoped her husband would explain everything to their daughter. She hoped one day she would see them again.

She listened to the street sounds quieten, heard the engine rev, the car accelerate. Behind her eyelids she imagined the journey, feeling and watching them turn, another junction, another road. She imagined the dust blowing up behind them, clogging the air, blocking out what lay behind.

She knew that soon the car would slow and turn off the main road; that it would stop, the engine would cut and the silence would embrace her. She knew where she would be.

She thought of the countless people who had travelled this way before her, and how few had made the journey back.

CHAPTER TEN

I don't remember the soldier leaving. I just remember the empty space where he had been, the cup of coffee untouched on the table, and my hope that I had imagined the whole thing.

That hot July night was the last I spent in my house, my home, Aziz asleep on the floor instead of my papa in his bed.

I laid in my room with no sleep coming, thinking of all the what-ifs and if-onlys. The conversations I'd had with Papa about leaving Iraq, how the answer was always the same. How I would see clouds skip across his eyes, and see them bring the mist in.

"We cannot leave yet," he would reply, "we must wait for Mama to return."

I had watched my papa miss my mama for nearly four

years. Only since the war began did I see him as a man missing his wife.

Who had shot him? Where had the bullet come from? A window? A roof? Had it been an Iraqi? A soldier? Why had Papa worked for these people? And I thought again about the American soldier. Surprised by him and his humanity.

Had it been worth it? Raiding that house? For so many deaths? I'd heard what people did to get to someone, to cause trouble, it happened all the time. Now, instead of reporting you to the Mukharabat, all they had to do was to mention the word 'terrorism' within American earshot and nod in someone's direction. That was enough to get your house ransacked, your belongings trashed and your family arrested and kept without charge.

That word flickered open eyes of American soldiers, made their nationality and their patriotism seep down their arms to their hands holding their weapons and their fingers resting on their triggers. A modern-day American taboo word. A word that draws breath deeper and quicker than any four-letter word could. I played the soldier's words over and over in my head. *Suspected* weapons dealer. My papa had died because of a *suspected* weapons dealer.

There was no easy segregation; the bad guys didn't all wear black and weren't all on the same side. This war, this *occupation*, had no lines drawn, still has no lines drawn. This is not yet a democracy in which we live.

Papa had told me he was scared for our future in Iraq, had said that if the country wasn't already in civil war then it sure as hell was on its way; he said he could see no end in sight, that things would get worse before they could even start to get better. And now he wouldn't see it, when finally, somewhere in the future, it was better.

I laid in the darkness, sleep avoiding me, trying to remember every conversation between me and Papa. Everything we had done together. Fix them permanently in my memory.

I remembered how people felt sorry for him after Mama left, how they were sympathetic, bringing us food or inviting us over. A man raising a child alone, how could he cope? Aziz took him out to coffee houses, and for walks along the banks of the Tigris. They talked in whispers, perched on edges of chairs, or in inconspicuous corners. When someone came near, they'd stop, light a cigarette and throw away a comment about our wonderful leader.

And I remember, will always remember, how much

he loved her. But as I wondered that last night I spent in my house, after he'd been killed, if now they were finally together, I felt lonelier and more vulnerable than ever before. Neither parents there to protect me. And I didn't want Mama to be dead, not because I didn't want them to be together, but because, selfishly, I didn't want to be alone.

And still with my eyes closed, my memory showed me those evenings me and Papa had spent together in the basement as bombs fell above us. I remembered marvelling over his stories, his voice lifting me from that dingy basement while the bombs fell and took me flying around this city in his time of youth. I flew over the markets as he ran through, a child of nine, chasing his friends. I hovered over street corners as my papa at twelve kicked a football through the neighbour's window. I glided through the golden sky as my twenty-two-year-old Papa smiled at a beautiful young woman with dark, shiny hair and green eyes, and gently took her hand.

His stories had filled my imagination, taken me away from the bombs and the guns, the screams and the crying. They had lifted me.

And I couldn't believe I would never see him again.

I wanted to speak to him. I wanted to ask him if it hurt, wanted to ask him if he was all right now, tell him that I missed him already, and that I loved him still.

I gave up on sleep; no peace, no calm to be found. From my bedside drawer I pulled a photo album and, tucking it under my arm, I wandered through the house in darkness, a little light peeking through windows, shadows and memories stretching across rooms. I stood in the kitchen, a drink in my hand, staring around at where my world had fallen apart only a few hours ago. My body ached with grief.

I headed to Papa's room, pulling aside the sheets, climbing into the empty bed. And as I opened the album, as I stared down at the photographs, old and faded, I again thought back to when he was alive. To when he pulled open an old box and took out this album that now sat on my lap.

And as I leafed through it, poring again over the photographs, it was as if he was sitting next to me, as if I could still hear his voice, and I could remember exactly what we'd shared that day.

"This is from when I was studying in London," he said. *"I*

took hundreds of photos, amazed at being in a different country, another culture to explore, with its history at my feet and in the air around me."

He turned to the middle of the book and I leaned forwards, squinting at the photographs, at the two people who smiled out at me.

"Is that Mama?" I asked.

He nodded. "That's where we met. I was in my last year. Your Mama, she was a year behind me. We'd both been living there a while, but only met when I had ten weeks left." He shrugged. "A wonderful ten weeks."

"But…"

"I know," he replied. "Over two thousand miles from home. What are the chances?"

His smile filled the room.

"We went everywhere together: the Tower of London, Hampton Court, Houses of Parliament, Buckingham Palace, Kensington Park, Piccadilly Circus. We spent days in museums and galleries, a grey afternoon in Trafalgar Square, rain running down Nelson's Column, bouncing off the lion statues; a bright morning in Hyde Park, waiting in the sunshine at Speaker's Corner to see who would be speaking, and getting heckled, and about what. For me, it was amazing, inspirational, shocking too, the freedom unimaginable to me before. The freedom to speak, act, think, travel, to hold opinions. At first I thought they must value and relish it so, but soon realised that they didn't; that was their way of life, the way they had known it for lifetimes. And I thought perhaps they puzzled over our lack of democracy and freedom as I did theirs."

He paused and looked away from his memories and back to me.

"It wasn't that English heritage, architecture, history… was better than Iraqi, it was just different, and new to me."

We pored over the pictures of them. Together. So young. So happy. "Mama looks so different. She's not wearing her necklace," I said to him, remembering the green stone reflecting the light, the gold around it sparkling.

"That was before I gave it to her," Papa replied.

He sighed and flicked the page over. "I should've shown you these years ago. I don't know why I didn't. Here."

He pushed the album to me, tapping his finger on a photograph. "Outside St Paul's Cathedral," he said with a smile. "A typical English day. Sunny, warm, grey, overcast, drizzly – all in one day. But a fabulous day for visiting the Cathedral."

I looked up from the photo to my papa, a lightness over his face, his expression lifted with his memories. I saw in his eyes that he wasn't in the room with me any more, he was back in time, twenty or so years, with his girlfriend, walking back into St Paul's Cathedral, in London. I stared at him, into his eyes, wanting to fall inside and look at his memories, listen to his memories.

"We'd been so busy with studying and exams that we'd done little but look at the inside of textbooks and journals for weeks on end. But finally I walked out of my last exam, out of the stuffy hall and into the sunshine where your Mama waited for me. With a mood as light as air, we laughed and joked as we walked from the university and on to a train, not knowing or caring where we were going; just letting the mood take us.

"We came out from the underground into a completely different London. As we drew our jackets around us and looked up to the grey clouds threatening rain, we saw the dome of St Paul's Cathedral and knew in an instant where we wanted to go.

"As we reached the steps we smiled at each other. A tourist took our photo. That photo. And seconds later the rain began. Great puddle-sized raindrops splashing on the white steps and the courtyard, pasting my hair to my head, squashing your Mama's curls. For a moment we just laughed, each watching the other becoming wetter and wetter. Then we ran inside.

"We fell into silence, the only sound was our shoes squelching on the marble floors. Why this building made such an impression on me, I don't know. I'd visited Nebuchadnezzar's

Palace, Abbassid Castle, Babylon, the Ishtar Gate, all of which, I'm sure, had an impact on me. But that day in June, something felt different.

"We climbed the steps to the whispering gallery, our hands clasped together, watching the windows above us darken as the thunder and lightning began. I felt exhilarated. But I felt safe. At the top, I let go of your Mama's hand, asking her to wait as I walked round to the other side, stopping when I was opposite her. I turned into the wall, closed my eyes and whispered, the words carried around to her. Slowly I turned, my eyes flicking across, looking for her, and suddenly she was next to me, and she leaned in to reply to my whisper with a smile and a kiss.

"For hours we shared views on Wren's architecture, read memorials, stared at tombs, marvelled over the history at our feet and our fingertips, and when finally we made our way outside, the sunshine had returned, stinging our eyes as they adjusted to the light.

"As we strolled through the streets of London, a strange sadness filled me. Sadness my studies had finished, sadness Iraq insisted I return so quickly, sadness at leaving this wonderful woman who walked at my side.

"I knew I would miss her; her smile, her laugh, her compassion and warmth and her company. But above all, just her. And as I watched the sunlight touch her make-up-free face and the breeze dance through her rain-splattered hair, I knew I would wait for her, and she for me. And I knew, when we finally saw each other again, what question I would be asking her.

"But at the same time I was worried. Would time blur away the edges of this love I felt for her? Would my memory be capable of holding on to it? Could my mind keep it fresh?

"I stared blankly into the window of a second-hand jewellery shop, and as I drew in a deep breath, determined to let nothing spoil this last day we had together for another year, my eyes came back into focus and I saw it. Staring up at me. An emerald; deep green, a sliver of orange, fine lines of black, speckles of gold. It was like staring into your Mama's eyes.

"And as she leafed through a bookshop a few doors ahead, I snuck in and bought it, not telling her, but holding it close and keeping it close all the time we were apart. A reminder not just of that day, not just of the time we had spent together, and not just of her eyes looking deep into mine. But a reminder of what we shared, of our love, of what we were together.

"Years later, after she'd returned to Baghdad and we'd met up again, when I'd asked her that question and she'd accepted, when you had been growing inside her all that time and had finally been born, I gave it to her. Made into a necklace now with filigreed gold circling it, I hung that green stone around her neck and told her its story. *And from that day, from when the nurse came into the room and took our first photograph together as a family, I never saw her without it. And I'm sure that she still has it now. Wherever she is.*

"You know, Lina, this war," he waved his hands around, "these Americans out on the street, the soldiers, I don't hate them, I see them in their heavy uniforms, heavy guns, struggling in the heat they're unaccustomed to, missing their families, their loved ones. I don't hate them for the conflict they've brought to our country. They're only following orders." He shrugged. He closed the album and pushed it towards me. "Keep it safe," he said.

As I sat in his bed that night he'd been killed, the photo album still on my lap, I wondered if he would blame the American soldiers now, if he would hate them now that he was dead. I cried as I turned the pages, wishing he was with me, and I missed him. I missed him. And I didn't know what to do to stop that terrible emptiness in my chest.

Through my blurry eyes I saw a loose photo slide out; Mama in bed. A bundle in her arms.

Papa at her side. Smiling.

And for the first time, that necklace was hanging around Mama's neck.

I placed the photo on the pillow next to me, Mama's pillow, and rested my head on the other. I felt the covers around me, holding me, and I imagined they were Papa's arms. And with my eyes closed I could smell him still on the pillow, and I imagined him with me, protecting me.

But still I felt alone.

I wished that the soldier had been mistaken, that he'd got the wrong man, that Papa would come through the door, that I would wake in the morning to the sounds of him singing in the bathroom, and the smell of cooking from the kitchen.

But I didn't.

The morning was hollow; the sunlight illuminating all the places Papa had once filled, but were now empty.

CHAPTER ELEVEN

The time after Papa died was like a blur, and as I think back to it now, I struggle to remember what happened. Life seemed unreal. The photo stayed with me, in my pocket, or at the side of my bed, my new bed in Aziz and Hana's house.

I remember his funeral; I remember holding that photo between my fingers as I stood outside the church, watching his coffin pulled out of the back of a van. Who had organised it? In this turmoil, how had they found someone to do a Christian service? And with all this death, how had they even found space in the graveyard? Everything seemed to pass me by.

I struggled to breathe, whether it was the stifling summer heat or the emotion thick around me. I stared at the coffin, a wooden box, a cross on top, so impersonal. I didn't want to believe my papa was inside.

I felt numb. I felt empty. All the emotion in me used up, an empty shell remaining.

I walked into the church with Hana on one side of me, Aziz on the other. I swallowed hard, lifted my chin, and kept my tears hidden. For now, at least. And although I stood at a pew at the front, I didn't hear a word of the service, I didn't want it to be real, didn't want to think of that moment every time I tried to remember Papa.

Instead I breathed in the calm of the place, the stillness and quiet. I ignored the service, my eyes scanning over the inside of the building, imagining how I would draw it, the smooth cream walls, the circular windows with their painted glass, the chandeliers dangling from the ceiling, the arches. What made it feel so calm? The architecture? The space? Or what it stood for?

And I looked over to the table at my side. Framed photographs of Papa, a wooden cross behind, candles in front, lit for him, the light flickering on to his face as he smiled out at me.

That's how I wanted to remember him, smiling at me, or his arms around me keeping me safe, or the warmth of his hand holding mine, or his kiss on my cheek as he wished me goodnight. All these things that I would never feel, never see, again.

In this dream state of memory I headed out of the church and the wind slapped me in the face, waking me and shocking me back to reality. I looked at the mourners standing around, nervous, knowing that a church was a dangerous place to be, and I saw them flick glances at people walking by. What were they looking for? Suicide bombers? Gunmen? Faceless people who now hated both Christians and anyone who dared to associate with us, wishing to rid Baghdad of us? Nothing was sacred any more. Not even a funeral.

But the people grieving for my papa weren't just Christians. And although I hadn't noticed them at the service and questioned whether they had dared go inside the church, I saw them now, so many of them, so many different people.

I saw Aziz, Layla's father, another neighbour, a friend of Papa's from university, all lift and support his coffin. What religion were they? I didn't care.

But it did matter.

Because they carried him through these streets of violence, of hatred, of discrimination and prejudice, of fear and retaliation and madness, whatever their religion or background or belief. With their friendship and love and respect, and with their fear of recriminations put to one side, if only for a short time, they carried my papa on their shoulders.

And at the graveside, with the heat bearing down upon me and the wind blowing sand and dirt into my face, my tears came. I thought of what I had lost. What had been taken from me. The most wonderful man. The most wonderful father. I couldn't even begin to find the words to describe my love for him, to describe the pride I held for him as I looked at the people around the graveside whose lives he had touched. And I thought of him, his life cut short, years stolen from him.

I realised he would never know what happened to Mama, would never again hold her in his arms. Nor would he ever know democracy in Baghdad, or see it again in peace time. And he would never see another sunrise, not even feel its heat upon his skin. And at that moment, as I stood at his grave, thinking of what his death meant to me, to him, to everyone he knew, I felt his loss more deeply than I had ever felt anything before.

I watched his coffin lowered into the ground, listened to the thud of the fresh soil landing on that wooden box below. I stood there, still, waiting, watching as people left, incapable of turning my back on Papa and walking away from him.

Then, suddenly, I glanced up and saw the American soldier moving towards me, his helmet and glasses off, his face bare. I was surprised; I didn't understand what he was doing there.

His eyes flicked to mine, down, then back again, and as he stopped in front of me, I knew I had nothing to say to him.

And even when he muttered "sorry", I knew I had no anger left to vent, no blame to lay. I was empty.

I think he thought I would speak to him, but I didn't. And eventually he left me on my own and walked out of the cemetery.

I stayed as the sun lowered and the light began to fade. The air was still, the sky above me turning from shades of blue, to lilac, to pink, to red. I stared around at other graves, white slabs sticking up out of the ground; some straight, some broken, some leaning, some with photos, some with flowers. They reached out into the distance. And beneath me was another. My papa.

I walked away feeling I was deserting him, still holding that photograph, staring down to my papa's smiling eyes, determined to remember him that way.

❖

The days and the weeks passed but I saw Papa still; on street corners, in shops, behind market stalls; a shadow, a familiar jacket or shirt, a similar hairstyle. And I would stop for a second, and would dare to look more closely.

I was always wrong. Of course. And always it hurt. But I hoped that in some way he was still watching over me and with my whole being, I missed him.

A few weeks later Aziz drove me back home to collect some things. The key thudded in the lock as I turned it, and the door creaked as I opened it. I stepped inside, the silence heavy, a strange air that wasn't fresh, everything just as I had left it that day. I strolled through the house feeling its emptiness, the sadness it seemed to hold now it had no one to fill it.

I rested my hand on Papa's bedroom door handle, pausing, feeling the coolness of it. *He's not in there*, I told myself. And I walked on. I packed up the things I wished to take to Aziz's house; some clothes, a few books, my old sketchpads, and that was it, all in a suitcase and one box.

I carried them to the kitchen where Aziz was waiting, and as he took the box from me, and we headed to the door, I stopped dead in my tracks. He looked at me, his eyes filled with the pity I was so used to seeing.

He patted me on the back. "Take some time," he said.

I watched him walk to the car, his eyes squinting against the sun, and left him to believe whatever he wanted. I headed down into the basement.

Light streamed through the little window, dust motes dancing in the air. I struggled through the boxes and over the mattress, left in case the bombing began again, and pulled a chair up to the wall.

I pulled the box out and opened it; all the money was still there. I wondered how safe it was. Whether it was better to leave the money here, or better to take it. If I left it here, would someone find it? Should I take it with me? I paused for a moment, thinking of thieves and bombs and Aziz and Hana's children. Eventually I pushed it back into the hole, and covered it with a broken brick.

That money was my hope; it gave me options and choices. I could leave the country, start afresh somewhere. I could travel, and see all those things I wanted to see. I could survive. I could live again. I moved the chair away, and leaned some junk against the wall; a yard brush, an old rug, a mop and bucket. I locked the door and took the key with me.

CHAPTER TWELVE

Life with Aziz and Hana was very different to my life with Papa. I used to enjoy my quiet times at home before Papa returned from work. I would sit and read a book, listen to music, sketch a little. I could do as I liked as long as dinner was made.

That was all gone.

Instead there was constant noise, chatter and bickering, and I was never alone.

Aziz was at work most days. Hana would go out for a while, selling things to the American troops: homemade food, cups of chai, things like that. They paid her well, and in dollars too. She no longer sent the boys to school; it was too dangerous, she said. When she went out I took care of the boys, but they were like limpets, clinging to me, demanding things: *Talk to me, read to me, play with me… Can I have something to eat? Can I have something to drink?* Again and again and again. And if I refused them, then they'd shout or scream at me.

So much happened every day. The city changed beyond recognition and so did my life. My birthday had passed, exams and results too. My application to university, despite Hana's protests, then the first day, new course, new people.

I wish Papa had been there to see it.

Every day Aziz drove me to uni, and every day he took me back home again. And while his wife tutted with her hands on her hips, shaking her head at the very idea I should be getting an education throughout this turmoil, or at all, Aziz simply replied that it was what Joe would've wanted.

I hoped university would offer some of the stability I longed for.

But still we fought for survival every day and still frustration ate away at me. There were so many stories of girls being abducted and held for ransom, their families forced to sell what little they had just for the hope of them returning. I remembered my friend Anita. Abducted yet returned when the ransom was paid. Although not the same person. Whatever had happened to her now kept her inside the house, fear ruling her.

Sometimes only a body came back. Sometimes nothing. Out of those two, I think I would have chosen a body. Not knowing what had happened to Mama – that was the worst thing.

There were explosions every day. More than once a day. Car bombs. Suicide bombers. Snipers. Seeing people killed was everyday life, the only question was how many were killed that day, or how many bodies you'd seen.

I loved being in class, listening, taking notes, trying to ignore the world outside the windows and forget the madness that waited for us all outside of those doors. But we couldn't forget, could we? Not completely. For it rested in our subconscious – the fear, the worry, the knowledge that you may not make it home that day, waiting for when your head wasn't filled with facts and figures, equations and problems.

It was hiding somewhere in my subconscious while I sat in a lecture room on the ground floor. I could hear people talking outside, see them strolling by. See the grass, green in places, patchy in others, the grey concrete paths, the short stubby bushes.

I felt safe in there. I felt happy, if only for that brief time.

But nowhere was safe and nowhere was impenetrable. Danger was in different degrees.

I remembered that, as the windows blew in, glass flying over us, a roar of noise, an explosion, the ground beneath us shaking. Books dropping off shelves and on to the floor, on to us as we dived to the ground for cover.

I heard screaming. Heard the crunch of glass under my feet and felt it press into my knees and my palms as I scurried for cover under the desks.

I waited. We all did. For shots through the window, for the ceiling to fall on us, for another explosion. Nobody spoke, nobody cried or screamed.

And the dust began to settle. And there were no shots, and the ceiling stayed up, and no more explosions rang out, on that day.

Crying from outside filtered through the empty window frames, and we lifted our heads up and looked at each other, brushing broken glass from our clothes and out of our hair, checking each other for injuries, calming each other, offering tissues or drinks of water, or just a comforting glance.

I picked out pieces of glass from one girl's face, her breath held as she tried to ignore the pain. And when I'd finished she bathed my cut knees and pulled a shard from the inside of my palm. Hospital was pointless. So many so much worse than us.

We stayed in the classroom as news came. Fearful of what we might find, or what might happen if we dared go out.

I seethed at the madness of it all. Angry that anyone would target a place of learning. But I was alive, and determined still to keep going, adamant that I would not let my dreams of university and my education and my career be destroyed.

But the attacks and the threats to the universities kept coming, and frustration clawed at me. For a while the university closed. Then lectures started again, but the timetables were constantly changed, trying to stop the insurgents from keeping track of when the classes were, trying to stop them targeting the students and the professors.

Still, I was determined to keep going.

I heard Hana talking one night. "Her place is at home," I heard her whisper.

"But life continues," Aziz replied.

"She needs to think of her future as a wife and mother," she argued.

"That's not what she wants."

"Going to university is too dangerous," was her response.

But I needed to hold on to this one thing sacred to me, my one hope. Because that was my escape from this world, and however dangerous it was, for as long as I possibly could, I would keep hold of it. Not let anyone – not soldiers with guns, not insurgents with bombs and most definitely not Hana with her words and opinions – take it away from me.

Hana didn't understand.

Hana, I was certain, didn't like me, didn't want me to have anything that was mine, didn't want to let me be myself. She barely looked at me, barely smiled or spoke to me. Why was she worried about me going to university? Was it because of the danger to me, or to Aziz? Him taking me back and forth to uni? But that didn't make sense. He drove his taxi every day. What difference would it make, two more trips? Why was my mama's sister convinced I should stay at home and prepare for becoming a wife and mother?

I wanted to go to classes, wanted to learn, wanted to study, wanted to see my friends, visit people in the evening, travel through the city. Normal, everyday, ordinary things.

Instead I learned what gun makes what kind of noise. I could tell you whereabouts in the city a bomb had gone off by the direction of the sound and the vibrations in the ground. I knew what IED and RPG stood for. I understood what the stripes on soldiers' uniforms meant.

These are not things I wanted to learn.

Every day there were roadblocks, checkpoints, curfews. Abductions, car-jackings, attacks, rapes, murders, lootings. Was this democracy? We could use the internet without fearing our every move was being watched, yet we had no electricity to use it.

I was living a nightmare.

And Layla, my best friend, barely spoke to me. I missed her smile, her gossiping about people we knew, boys she had spoken to. Her infectious laugh that could cheer me from the greatest gloom. At university, hers was a friendly face in a sea of unknowns, but she avoided me. When lectures were on, she wouldn't sit with me. When they finished she would rush off to avoid my company. It was the same with most of the people in my class, but I knew why and I understood.

Fear.

CHAPTER THIRTEEN

Whatever happened to Sacha? Part II

BAGHDAD. A WOMEN'S PRISON. NOVEMBER 1999

Sacha sat on the end of the mattress, her body squashed between two others, her legs drawn in. She still wore the suit from her last day at work a month ago. But the pink blouse no longer smelt of the perfume she had sprayed, and the grey trousers no longer held the crease down the front, and the jacket no longer made her feel smart and important.

Because now the armpits were circled with sweat, her blouse and trousers stained with her own blood and vomit, and covered in dust and dirt. The stench of the cell clung to the fibres. The smell of fear and pain, disbelief and misery. The smell of disappearing hope.

She tucked a strand of greasy hair behind her ear and glanced at the women around her, some dressed in abayas, one in a night-gown, all in the clothes they had been taken in.

Her eyes peered through the gloom of the cell at the fifteen women crammed into a space meant for six. She had counted them when she had arrived, not one had been released since. No visitors, no exercise, no phone calls, no lawyers, no rights. She knew none of the relatives of the prisoners would know where they were, would have been told even if they had asked.

"What have I done?" she questioned over and over in her head. "What was my crime? To refuse to work for them? Was that it?" But she knew it was, and knew that was all it took; knew, as she looked at all the other women in there with her, that it could take even less.

She waited every day, in hope and in fear, for the door to be opened. "Maybe I'll be released. Allowed a phone call. Speak to Joe, to Lina." But the door was opened only for food – rice, stale bread, water – or to shout a name.

That day she didn't hear the footsteps, or the key in a lock, or see the door open, and didn't have time to think whether to lift her eyes to the guard in hope of food, or hide away in fear of the unknown. She just heard her name, issued from the large, uniformed man in the doorway, a glint in his eye, a smirk dancing on his lips.

"Sacha."

Her legs lifted, her body moved. Unwilling, yet accepting. She prayed for the time to pass quickly. She prayed for mercy. Fifteen pairs of eyes watched her go, pity filling the room with a guilty appreciation that it wasn't them.

Dread enveloped her as she was led into another room. Her eyes scanned over the blood stains on the walls, the whip in the corner, the hook hanging from the ceiling, the machine in the middle, the wires and clips, the chair with straps and buckles.

She was asked nothing. For no names, no excuses, no reasons, no apologies. A clip was attached to her toe, another indenting the flesh of her ear.

And there was no warning.

She screamed.

Pain coursed through her, up her body in waves, her muscles tightened, her body stretching, her head thrown back.

It stopped. And she breathed.

And it came again.

Tearing and growing and clawing through her body. The pain like an animal stretching inside her.

She shouted. She screamed.

She drifted in and out of consciousness. She thought of her life and she remembered her past, visions of it returning to her in waking dream, in hallucination – walking the streets of London with Joe, swimming in the river with her beautiful daughter.

She drifted back. Her eyes lifted open, but the room and the people in front of her were blurred, doubled, her vision incoherent. She watched a darkened shape move towards her. She didn't see the fist raise, or see it come down. She felt the chair slip sideways underneath her and felt her head hit the concrete floor.

She had no strength left. She felt unconsciousness chasing her, grappling up, darkening and diminishing what vision she had. On the floor she could make out a puddle of deep red; sticky, drying and hardening. A boot stood in it, the toes lifting up and down.

She slipped away.

A baby in her arms. A flurry of dark hair. Pinkened cheeks and a frown. Warmth and happiness in her chest. A man at her side. His smile drunk with exhilaration. A kiss from him.

And a kiss on the baby's forehead.

"Lina?" he asks. "After your grandmother?" She nods, smiling. She looks to the baby.

"Lina," she replies. He pulls a box from a pocket. Offers it to her. A necklace, green stone, filigreed gold. She feels it around her neck.

She peeled her eyes open and saw faces peering down at her, concern and tears filling their eyes. She felt the women lift her, felt them place her on to the mattress in the cell, felt them tend to her as they dabbed her head, and cooled her body.

Is it a sin to wish for death? she thought. *Could I do that to my family? Leave them? Abandon them?*

What have I done?

She thought of Lina, of Joe, and how selfish she had been. She should have taken the job, done whatever the authorities wanted.

What if they go after my family? she thought. *What if they torture them? What if they kill them?* Her head swam with a thousand should haves and if onlys. She wanted her family. She wanted to tell them to leave the country. Leave and head for safety.

She prayed and wished with every inch and every breath and every heartbeat. She pictured her husband's face in front of her and told him over and over and over to leave, to take Lina, to escape. Her imagination shouted and begged and pleaded.

CHAPTER FOURTEEN

Classes at university began again and I felt the warmth it gave me, the lightness it brought to my step, and the smile that almost dared to creep on to my face. It gave me optimism and hope, it was something to wake me in the mornings, to lift my eyelids, to make my lungs breathe in and remember to exhale.

But my hope of it bringing some normality was naive. It was the end of the second day back, and I shoved my books into my bag, and left the room. It was only a short walk to where Aziz picked me up, and as I strolled across the campus, my thoughts were still in my lecture and mulling over my homework.

Did I walk past any of the men with guns? Would I have noticed them? Instinct made me duck as the first shot echoed out. I threw myself to the floor. I could tell it came from behind me, not far away. I glanced back, but couldn't make sense of the scene behind me, people running, or on the floor, screaming and shouting and crying.

I thought I could make out Aziz's car and I stood up and ran. I didn't stop to find out if anyone was injured. I didn't stop to help. I just ran. And my lungs burned, and my legs trembled, but fear and adrenalin forced me on to the car as gunfire sounded around me.

And I was alive.

And this was normality in this city, I realised, as I sat in the car, shaking, sucking in breath, so scared, so relieved. Gunfire and car bombs, IEDs and death threats. It was not expecting to be home for dinner, it was knowing you may not make it to lunch. Death wasn't a word reserved for the old or the ill, it was a reality everybody faced every minute of every day.

The next morning I stood in the bathroom, staring into the mirror while I brushed my teeth, summoning up the courage to keep going, convincing myself that it wouldn't happen again.

Hana opened the door. "You're not going to university any more," she announced. "You can stay at home and help me."

I stared at her with a toothbrush hanging from my mouth, confused, hoping I had heard her wrong.

"Where did an education get your Mama? And your Papa? Didn't do them any good, did it? Nearly got you killed yesterday too."

I had no reply for her. I couldn't believe what I was hearing. I waited for Aziz to comment, to tell her she was wrong, that having an education didn't cause the death of Mama and Papa.

But his eyes stayed low, and no reply came from him.

There was no discussion, just her decision. I found my voice and stuttered an argument; I couldn't just stop, I'd be thrown off the course, I wouldn't graduate, I wouldn't become an architect, I wouldn't be able to support myself.

"You should be thinking of finding yourself a suitor," she said. "Someone to take care of you now your father's gone. He should never have filled your head with nonsense about studying and careers. Your place is at home, looking after your family, your husband and your children. As your Mama should've."

My mouth hung open in disbelief as she turned to me, a look in her eye I couldn't quite fathom. Was it anger or hatred or despair even?

"And I told your Mama that," she continued. "I told her she was a fool, that her family would suffer because of the decisions she'd made, but she didn't listen, and look at where it got her. Got her killed, didn't it?"

"You don't know that," I managed to mutter. "You don't know she's not alive."

She scoffed at me. "Don't be a fool, Lina. Don't be like your father. All this rubbish about *when* she comes back. She hasn't come back in all this time, Lina, because she's dead. I knew it, have known it for years, as you should've. As your Papa should've. And all this rubbish about the necklace. Do you really believe that? That because it hasn't miraculously made its way home, or he hasn't found it in some second-hand shop, that it must still be with her? That she must be alive somewhere? It's rubbish, Lina, and it was wrong for your Papa to make you believe it. He was living in a dream world, and it's about time *you* woke up." She paused, and I stood, shell-shocked. My chest burning with anger, but I could find nothing to say.

"While you're living with me, you'll do as I say. I say you will no longer attend university, you will tell them that you're not going back. Instead you can help around the house. You can earn your keep."

I was empty. I had no words. I prayed that Aziz would persuade her to change her mind, but although I heard them talking that evening, there was no retraction of her orders.

I didn't understand Hana. I didn't understand how she could be happy and satisfied with her life. She got up early before everyone else, she prepared meals, she cleaned, she tidied, she shopped for food, she cooked, she looked after the children. And it was the same every day. And it had been even before the war. No end in sight, no change, no working towards a goal apart from her children growing up and leaving home. How could she not be bored?

That night, I couldn't sleep. I got up and went downstairs, stood at the window and listened to the sound of gunfire.

I wanted to hear the sounds that used to fill the skies of Baghdad; the hustle and bustle of traffic, the chatter of people, but as I closed my eyes, all I could hear was the interminable drone of generators. Like bees. One stuck in each house. The only way you could guarantee being able to cook or wash clothes, turn the fan for relief from the heat, or watch television. But only if you had fuel. I wanted it to stop. I wanted quiet. I wanted peace.

And as I stood there with my hands over my ears, I felt Aziz's hand on my shoulder, asking me what was wrong.

"Hana hates me," I said.

"She's angry," he sighed. "But not at you. She's been angry for a long time." We stared out across the city. "You know what happened at the shelter? At Amiriyah, during the last Gulf War?"

I nodded. How could I forget about that? How could anyone?

"She lost all her family there. All but your Mama, that is. She's scared that more of her family will be taken. She loved your Mama desperately. But they never understood each other. Hana never understood your Mama's ambition, or her desire for a career. She missed her terribly when she went to England. Hana's views are simple. We married and she wanted to stay at home, even before the boys were born. She felt that was her place. That's what she wanted from life. When that job offer came for your Mama, it was discussed quietly through the family; what it would mean to work for them, what could happen, what turning it down might bring.

"Hana's reasoning in her head was very simple; the dilemma wouldn't exist, the possible threat to Sacha's life, and perhaps the family, if Sacha hadn't studied, hadn't gone to university, hadn't wanted a career.

"Hana told her she should be glad to be alive and keep a low profile. But that's not what Sacha wanted. She was headstrong, Lina. You know that. But when she went missing... imagine what that did to Hana. And then what happened to your Papa..."

"But that's not my fault," I replied.

He smiled at me and stood up. "Come on," he said, and he took my hand and led me back upstairs. He picked up a framed photograph. "Who's that?" he asked.

I stared at the faces. "Mama and Hana," I said.

He nodded. "Do you ever look in the mirror?"

My reply was a frown.

"When Hana looks at you she sees Sacha, your Mama, her missing sister, staring back. She struggles, Lina. Think of the life she's had. Losing so many people close to her. Scared something would take your Mama and Papa away from her as well. Then it did."

He paused watching my face. "Try not to be too hard on her."

I took the photo into my room, looking from it, to the mirror, and back. I could see it now, everything, the hair, the face shape, the mouth. But not the eyes; mine were brown like Papa's. I wondered how it had been for Papa; I wondered if, when he looked at me, he saw Mama staring back.

I tried to understand Hana. But I had changed so much to fit in. I gave up my time to look after the boys, I did as much as I could around the house, and now I would be dropping out of university. I felt a burden and a let-down. Every day I missed Papa and every day I wished for Mama to return. I prayed to leave this place, to get my life back again, to live again, to breathe again.

❖

That night, I took out a map of the world. I unfolded it and laid it across the sheets and looked at the countries and thought of where I could go, where would be safe. I could study abroad, I thought, then return to help rebuild my country. The money would help, but my education was the key to everything. I could have a profession. Then I would have options and choices, could make plans for the future.

I prayed that night, to a God whose ears seemed to be troubling him, that I would hear from Mama soon. Because although there was no longer Papa to keep hope alive that she would return, and Hana had given up on her, I would not. I prayed for her safety. And I knew it was a miracle I was asking for, but I needed something to hold on to, I needed to see her again.

Yet it was not Mama who came back into my life, soon after that.

It was someone else.

Someone I could never have expected.

CHAPTER FIFTEEN

I resigned myself to the life I would have at Hana and Aziz's. For now, at least. I accepted I would not be going to university. I had to, there was no choice. Aziz convinced Hana to let the boys go to school though, and every day circled around survival; the boys arriving at school safely, returning home safely; Aziz surviving another day driving his taxi, trying to earn some money; Hana finding food, there being enough power to cook, water to drink, to wash, to clean.

Aziz kept me sane. I felt the air suck from the room whenever he left. His over-sized, boisterous friendliness was an infectious disease. A massive teddy-bear of a man, who I wished I could tuck under my arm and carry with me all day.

Without him, I would fall to pieces.

I helped around the house and some days we took food and drink to the American soldiers to sell. It made a bit of money, but not much. After a while some would wait for us, they knew who we were; they liked Hana's cooking and praised her on it. But it scared me, talking to them. I was scared they would steal from us, attack us, ridicule us. And seeing them reminded me of Papa. The memory and the pain still so real, so raw.

They spoke no Arabic, knew little of our customs and culture, and were clumsy in their dealings with Iraqis. A little knowledge and understanding would've gone a long way.

I kept my head down and I listened to them. Kept my eyes low and my opinions hidden.

But there was one, who always stayed towards the back when I arrived, who never caught my eye, never took off his dark glasses or his helmet, never offered a smile. Never looked at me. But despite this, and despite my feelings of guilt and fear, I looked forward to seeing him. There was something about him that drew me to him, some familiarity, something in his demeanour, something about that small part of his face that wasn't obscured, that was familiar.

But it scared me, thinking that, because my very

being screamed at me that it was wrong to want to see him. These soldiers were occupying my country, walking around with guns, pointing them at civilians, stalking around in mirrored sunglasses, cigarettes drooping from corners of mouths. Arrogant. Insolent.

Yet this one I dared to think I might like. And after a few days of seeing him at the gas station, I headed over to him and he finally spoke, greeting me in Arabic fashion.

"Asalaamu aleikum," he said.

I looked at him, surprised. "Wa aleikum asalaam," I replied.

I had my beliefs about America and their soldiers. He did not fit these beliefs. American soldiers did not greet us in Arabic.

I scanned his face, his eyes obscured by his dark glasses, his face creasing as he gave a quick, flickering smile.

I felt confused. He thanked me for the food, said it was delicious, and said he hoped I would come and see him again the next day. I kept my mouth shut. He didn't know I could speak English, and I felt something of a spy as I listened to these men.

The following day he was there again, still wearing

his dark glasses, and when Hana moved away I walked towards him, my stomach lurching, my face flushing and burning and my hands shaking as I handed him a cup of chai.

I willed the courage to speak to him in English, to let down my defences. "Why are you guarding the gas station?" I whispered.

He looked at me from the corner of his eye. "Well, just to make sure there's no trouble. Y'know, because it's rationed, and there are huge queues." He shrugged. "People get frustrated. Annoyed. Tempers get frayed."

And he paused, turned his head and looked at me. Really looked at me. And I felt so uncomfortable that I took a step back, hanging my head, my hair falling in front of my face.

"Your Joe's daughter, aren't you?" he whispered. He took off his dark glasses and lifted down his helmet. And the shock of it took my breath away. I swung around to him, staring up to his face, my mouth hanging open, my face a deep frown.

"I'm Steve," he said, extending his hand. But I couldn't take it. I couldn't touch him. "I came to your house that day," he continued. "And the funeral."

I was about to shake my head.

But I looked at him properly now. My eyes searching past the stubbled chin, flicking over his dusty blonde hair, his narrow face, those eyes, those bright blue American eyes, filled with compassion I thought no soldier could hold, and I saw him, the soldier who had given me such bad news, and despite the heat of early summer, I felt cold. Every inch of me prickled. The hurt and pain of that day and every day since, without Papa, flooded back and I gulped away tears.

"I recognised you a while ago," he continued, "but I didn't think you'd want to see me, so I tried to keep away."

I watched him as he hid his head again inside the helmet, obscured his eyes and face again behind those glasses, but now I could still see him. I could see him sitting at my kitchen table, see his fingers edging the cup in front of him, hear those words coming from his mouth as he told me Papa had been shot.

I watched the Steve in front of me lift the cup to his mouth, watched him drink, watched his dusty fingers and broken nails wipe the corners of his mouth.

"It's nice to see you," he said, holding the empty cup out to me.

I didn't have any words to say, couldn't get them past

the lump in my throat and the burning in my chest. I nodded and reached out for the cup. But for a second, he didn't let go.

"I'm sorry," he whispered, "about your dad, Joe."

And I looked up at him. "I'm sorry for hitting you," I breathed.

He smiled and let go, a shrug on his shoulders. And as I turned away from him, I felt my cheeks flush, and as I walked away, I looked up and saw Hana's eyes boring into me.

I thought about Steve that night as I lay in bed, but I didn't want to. I didn't want to think of how he made me feel. That, I was going to ignore. He was an American. An American soldier. Above all else, that was his label; that was his business here.

The next day Hana sent me by myself. And I told myself I was going for Hana, because she wanted me to. And as I walked there I told myself I was feeling nervous because it was dangerous, because of the bombs on street corners and guns hiding inside windows, not because of the idea of looking again into his blue eyes.

And when I arrived, I told myself that my stomach was turning because I was so relieved I was safe, and as I saw Steve again, as I poured his drink, my hands were shaking because I was pleased to be earning Hana some money.

I sat with him in the shade while he drank, and all the caution I had told myself to exercise diminished as we talked. He showed me photos of his family he kept in his pockets; his parents and his sister, Maggie who, he said, was the same age as me and studying at university.

I stared at the photo of her and felt an overwhelming jealousy: to be allowed and able to go to university. I had promised myself I wouldn't speak to him about my life, about me, yet I found I was telling him everything; about Mama going missing, Papa before the war, having to stay with Hana and Aziz, not being able to study.

He made me feel so comfortable it was like seeing an old friend again. It was as if we had known each other for years.

He asked me questions about living here, about what it was like before, if it was better now. And I spoke more honestly than I ever had about life and about my disappointment at the present and my trepidation about the future.

He told me that if he could, he would pick me up from the house every day and drive me in a tank to university, then later he would take me home again.

He made me smile, and I think it was the first smile to touch my face in a long time. Its warmth spread down me and I wondered if I'd made a friend. I hoped I had. It was the most I had talked to anyone in months and months. It was the most I had ever talked to a man who wasn't family, yet oddly, the thought of him being male never entered my head. He was someone to speak to and to share thoughts with.

But he was an American soldier.

We fell silent and I realised how long I'd been talking, how much I'd told him, how many questions he'd asked, and for a moment there was a gap between us that neither of us seemed to know how to fill.

In silence still, I gathered together my things and packed them away, and as I paused, not knowing how to say goodbye, he took off his sunglasses and looked at me.

"Let me take you somewhere," he whispered.

I didn't move, I just stared at him, confused and shocked. Speechless.

"Just for a few hours. Let me take you out of the city. Take you somewhere… oh, I don't know… somewhere peaceful."

I scoffed at the word, at the suggestion even. "That's impossible," I replied.

"Maybe not," he said.

"How?"

He shrugged. "I don't know. Not yet. Let me see what I can work out. See what we could do, where we could go."

And suddenly I felt scared, the reality of the situation crashing on to me. "I can't do that," I said, moving away, shaking my head, my hands trembling.

He frowned.

"You're a soldier. And you're American," I said. "That's it. There is nothing else. I shouldn't have come. I shouldn't have spoken to you. I shouldn't have told you about me." I turned, striding away, leaving him standing alone.

And I felt so angry as I walked home. Why did he have to say that? Why did he have to spoil things? I wanted to be able to look forward to the next day, to seeing him again, to chat with him again. I wanted to feel that elevation and excitement that I hadn't felt for as long as I could remember.

But now? Now he had said that, it all seemed so much more real.

I knew this friendship, if that's what it was, couldn't last. I knew what he was suggesting could never happen;

that mouths would gossip and fingers would wag. Decent Iraqi girls do not fraternise with American soldiers, and just talking to him was risking bringing shame on the family, and making a name for myself. It was thoughtless and it was dangerous and I knew I must remember what happened with Papa, and how his relationship with the soldiers was seen, that maybe he was killed for it. I knew I couldn't go anywhere with Steve. Yet I longed for a friend to be with, to speak with, to share things with.

Was that so wrong?

At the house there was no one to talk to. Hana hated me. Aziz was never there, and when he was, he was tired, or worried, or wanting to be with his wife and children. He always had a smile for me, and I knew he cared, but where before Aziz had always been the epitome of fun and laughter, slowly it seemed to be leaving him. I missed his booming laugh and his huge smile.

So many smiles were lost in the war, and so many tears were found.

I thought about what I had found, what had found me. This American soldier. This strange thing appearing from out of nothing but anguish and turmoil and destruction and fear and hatred. He gave me something different. He was a breath of fresh air to me.

But he was dangerous. Or would be, if I kept seeing him. And his suggestion? It frightened me. I knew I couldn't go anywhere with him. That it could never happen. Then why, why did the mere idea of it keep coming to my head? Why, when I closed my eyes, did I still see him?

Why did I think of him when everything to do with him was impossible?

CHAPTER SIXTEEN

Whatever happened to Sacha? Part III

What hell is this? Sacha thought.

She kept count of the days as November, December and January disappeared inside the cell. She knew it was February 16th when she was called out for the last time; day number one hundred and ten. She had been beaten, raped and tortured.

The same clothes still hung off her, stained with food and vomit, sweat and urine. But she wasn't ashamed of how she looked and smelled. She was ashamed of her weakness when she cried for her husband to rescue her, her mother to hold her tight, and her daughter to cuddle in her arms. She was ashamed of the screams which ripped through her when she could take the pain no longer.

And when the torture finished, she would think, *Am I lucky for being alive? Lucky is making it to the house a second before the rain comes. Lucky is dropping your car keys near a grate and them not falling in. Lucky is finding a 250-dinar note lying motionless on the dusty ground.*

Being alive is not luck. Being alive is a right.

As she walked barefoot from the cell that last time, she wondered if this would be the time she would die. *Wouldn't that be better?* she thought. *For death to release me from this?* She accepted what would happen next, she prayed for it to end and with her eyes low, she watched her feet shuffle towards that room.

But when the guard led her past it, she woke a little, felt her breath quicken, her face flush, her palms sweat.

He paused to unlock a door, and Sacha struggled to keep the idea out of her head that she might be being released. His fingers squeezed into the purple bruises around the top of her arm and dragged her forward. Another guard joined them, keys spinning around his finger, and another set of boots walked their way. She heard a key click in a lock, the heavy creak of a door.

And sunlight drenched the room. She screwed her eyes up, a greeny orangey hue dancing behind her eyelids. The heat hit her as she was dragged outside, her toes scuffing on the concrete, loose gravel pressing into her heels. She breathed in, sucking in the fresh air, new smells coming to her nose, new sounds to her ears. She eased one eye open a crack, desperate to see more than concrete and walls.

A man barked at her, ordering her on to the back of a truck. But with her wrists tied together and her body weak, she could barely lift her arms. She felt herself pulled upwards, felt the strain in her shoulders as she was dragged up by the rope around her wrists and thrown on to the truck, her elbow skidding across the floor, her head stopping the momentum as it hit a metal bench.

Sacha didn't move.

She woke to find herself surrounded by people. Prisoners sat with her, all silent, fearful of where they were going, what was to happen next.

She breathed heavily, sucking in the fresh air, the smell of the desert, a faint scent of wild flowers somewhere in the distance.

Am I being released? she dared to think.

The engine stopped, a prisoner spoke. "Thank you for travelling with me," he said. "I wish you all luck. Inshallah."

He bowed his head. And for a few moments before

they were dragged and pulled and ushered off the truck, a silence fell, heavy with trepidation; fear of the unknown and fear of the fate that waited for them.

The heat was white, silver, molten. It willed her to close her eyes. She thought of the cell she had left that morning; she thought of opening a fridge door on a hot day, exhaling cool, damp air; she thought of her father standing on the banks of the Tigris, pulling off his shirt, his belly hanging over his trunks, the layer of sweat on his body, collecting on his brow, in his moustache. She remembered him jumping into the water, feeling the cool drops as they splashed on to her skin. How old had she been? Five? She remembered telling her mother of that memory as they sat together in the shelter.

"How do you remember that?" her mother had asked, shaking her head.

Sacha wobbled on her feet, the heat punishing her, torturing her, bringing forward memories long forgotten. *What would my mama think of me now?* she questioned. *What would she say to me?* And she imagined her holding her in her arms, rocking her gently, whispering in her ear.

The prisoners stood in a line. How many? She couldn't remember.

A shot rang out. Sacha jumped, looking round,

checking herself, checking she was breathing. She saw a man at the beginning of the line, fallen to the floor, his face in the dirt, a trickle of blood leaking on to the ground.

And another shot. No cry, no shout, no scream. Just a thud.

And another.

She counted them. That was the third. She felt panic in her skin, her body, her blood. *What number am I?* she thought.

Shot number six rang out. Another thud. Closer this time.

Am I number seven? she thought.

She kept her eyes down, watching her own feet as she gently moved her toes in the sand, feeling the grains between them, tiny indentations where they rested. A line of crimson crept into her field of vision, crept along the floor towards her feet. Fear rose in her chest. She moved her head slightly, her eyes reaching out to the left, searching for the owner of the blood. Wanting to know, but not wanting.

She saw him.

Number six was lying dead next to her. The man who had wished them all luck.

She *was* number seven.

A strange calm fixed over her.

She lifted her head and looked the gunman in the eye. She watched him load his weapon, watched the bullet that would kill her drop into the chamber. She watched him raise his right arm, steady it with his left, his head leaned to one side, his left eye closed, his right looking through the sights, down the barrel, across the yard.

To her. Straight into her eyes.

She didn't look at the finger on the trigger, she kept both eyes fixed on her killer.

She saw his deep brown eyes, his thick eyelashes, a mole on the side of his nose.

She waited.

She watched the man open his left eye, straighten his head, lower his arms. He grinned at her. A grin of power, of hatred. "Maybe not today," he said.

Then a bang, and a thud.

Number seven lay on the floor.

Sacha was number six and a half.

Out of the twenty prisoners on the truck, fifteen lay dead on the ground in a sandy field next to a tall concrete building. They were all shot in the head.

Sacha stood in a sea of bodies.

With spades in their hands, the five survivors chipped away at the earth with the little energy they had left, none muttering a word, all immersed in their own shock and grief, and guilty sense of relief.

CHAPTER SEVENTEEN

I had no intention of going out the next day, no intention of seeing Steve, no intention of speaking to anyone but Hana and Aziz and the children, or staring at anything but the four walls that held me.

I volunteered to look after the boys, or to clean the house, or to do the washing, but it was all refused. Instead I was told to return again to the gas station, and my face fell as I realised it was impossible to hide from whatever was going on inside my head.

I took my sketchbook with me this time, deciding I would stop on the way, draw how we now had to live. And I ignored the danger around me, that I was being more than thoughtless for merely being out alone, and I really looked at, and really saw, what had become of my city.

I stepped around rubble, over holes in roads, dodged missing pavements and felt like I was walking on the surface of the moon. My pencil wasn't used to drawing rubble, or buildings with only three walls left, or shops with no fronts. The architect in me wanted to sketch order and precision, purpose and beauty, because that's what my country had.

Before.

While I tried to get these images on paper, I thought of who had done this, I thought of the insurgents and their IEDs and grenades, I thought of the soldiers and their bombs and guns. And I thought of Steve; an American, a soldier.

My feet crunched beneath me and I stopped. I glanced down: shards of glass, coloured glass, covering the tarmac, chunks of rubble, lumps of concrete around me. I looked up to where the church had been, that was now laying in pieces at my feet. Yet another space in the landscape, but not quite, just its bones remaining, stretching up into the sky. I could sketch what I could see, but couldn't capture the feeling; incapable of showing how the stained glass on the ground used to sparkle into life when the sun hit it, and the rubble on the floor used to be walls that held together something special for so many.

And inevitably my feet led me to the gas station.

I sat down opposite, hidden in a corner, obscured from view, the overhang of a building providing a little shade. And I watched. And I sketched. A snapshot of my city, my home, what it had become.

How many cars were waiting, queuing to fill up? I could count seventy-two, but they faded into the distance, disappeared around a corner and the dust and their muted colours blended one into another, the end invisible and unknown. A few cars were topped with yellow taxi signs, and I wondered if Aziz was driving one of them.

What a simple thing this once was and what a difficult thing it had now become. I sketched the trucks, the cars, the vans, the lorries, but couldn't get the emotion of the drivers, the fear that pulled down their mouths and wrinkled their brows. The knowledge of events that had passed here; car-jackings, stabbings, robberies, and no possibility of leaving quickly. Twelve hours to wait, maybe. Why should they be scared of filling their cars? Why should this be life-threatening? But now, here, in this city, just to live was life-threatening, wasn't it?

The thought took me back to the soldiers.

I watched them.

They had all looked the same to me before, in their camouflage jackets and trousers, their heavy boots and dark glasses. Guns in their arms and pads on their knees, straps and cables and wires stretching around their chests.

But now, I saw Steve.

For a moment I stopped, watching him, thinking about him. And as I dodged across the road, I saw him look my way, saw him mutter something to his colleague before turning to me, his eyes on mine, a smile inside them. I tucked my sketchbook into my bag and poured him a drink.

"I didn't think you'd come back again," he said, taking a sip.

"Neither did I," I whispered. I glanced to him, watching his fingers on the cup, his eyes darting over the cars in front of him, the people, the other soldiers. Then to me.

"I didn't mean to upset you. It was a stupid idea, hell I shouldn't've even thought it. But…"

I shook my head. "No, it… it was… nice. Just… unexpected." I had surprised myself. By coming back, by wanting to see him, wanting to speak to him, spend time with him, by even thinking, to myself, that yes, I would like to go somewhere with him. Yes, take me somewhere away from here. Somewhere peaceful. But how could I say that?

Still I kept coming back to that same thing: what he was.

We stood in silence, next to each other, with each other, not touching, not looking, but ever so slightly too close. Nervousness or excitement or something that wasn't fear for a change, prickled at my skin and leaped in my chest. What was I doing?

Nothing, I told myself. *Nothing.*

Very slowly and very quietly he tilted his head towards me, flashing his bright blue eyes to mine. "But if you did change your mind," he began, "then we could go somewhere, if you wanted, together." He shrugged and I heard him swallow hard. "Not as a *date*, but as two people who get along and would like to spend some time together where there's less of a chance of getting shot. Or blown up."

I didn't say a word.

"I don't know where we'd go, or what we could do, but y'know, I could sort something out. I could get a couple of hours free."

I lifted my head and looked at him. I didn't know what to say. I didn't know what to do. I knew it was dangerous. I knew some people would think it reckless. Some would think I was a traitor. But for a moment, just a moment, I put all that aside and looked at the man standing before me.

And I nodded. "Yes," I breathed.

"Yes?" he frowned.

"Let's go somewhere, do something." And I tried to smile, but caution and fear kept it hidden. Fear of what I was getting myself into, where this was going to lead, the danger I was putting myself in, and my family. I knew how senseless it was, not just agreeing to go somewhere with him, but the feeling I had for him, the emotion, the friendship, the attachment that was growing, it was all pointless.

But I couldn't help it and I couldn't stop it. And when I could find the courage not to listen to my fear, I would tell it I didn't care.

For nearly a week I saw Steve every day and I began to feel a new freshness, something to look forward to when I went to bed at night, a reason to get up in the morning. Although still I was scared, of whatever it was between us.

My head questioned Steve's motives for being so friendly, but it had been so long since I'd felt anything *but* anger and frustration and fear and loneliness that I tried to ignore that part of me. Instead I welcomed the feeling of warmth in my chest and how a smile felt to my face.

I would make chai in the morning, and take it down in a flask, making sure I offered it to other soldiers as well. But I would offer it to Steve last, and as he drank we would talk. And we talked about everything and anything; about the architecture of Iraq and American history, our favourite films and books, music we liked to listen to, places we longed to visit, rollercoasters and soggy popcorn, sweets you couldn't buy any more and favourite toys that had long since broken.

And too often we would pause and find that we were standing too close to each other, or looking at each other for too long, or my laugh would be too loud, or I would reach out to touch him as you would touch your hand to a friend's arm, and I would remember the danger I was in, and what people would think and say and do.

But still every day I walked to see him, and every day I waited for him to say that he had sorted something out, that he was taking me somewhere.

When I was walking to him and when I was with him, I didn't care about the danger, but when I left, I felt eyes upon me, frowns glaring at me, and heard whispers of *gahob, whore,* of *feaky-feaky, sex.*

"Come and entertain us," a different soldier shouted.

"How much?" another asked.

And I felt my face flush and wished I could hide it.

But I haven't done anything wrong, I kept thinking. *Why should I deny myself this small piece of happiness?* But still the echo of what Steve was bounced in my head; he was an American, he was a soldier; America bombed my country, destroyed my city, occupied my home. But, and there were so many buts, Saddam was gone, the man who took my mama from me, and so much had been promised for our futures: freedom, democracy, a better life.

By the end of our week, it felt as if we'd known each other for years, yet we had barely spoken for half an hour each day. I felt I was becoming myself again, felt my heart smile and my body lighten.

"Meet me tomorrow?" he said as I emptied out the dregs from the flask I was carrying.

I stopped and stared at him.

"I've got some time. Couple of hours in the afternoon,"

he whispered. "Think I know where we can go."

I didn't reply.

"Meet me up there." He nodded down the road. "Near the liquor store."

Still I struggled for words. Thinking. Could I do this? Really? I shook my head. "No," I said, my voice quavering, "not there, someone will see me."

Another soldier walked past him, patting him on the back. "C'mon," he said.

Steve looked at me. "Lina, I've got to go."

"Come to the house," I muttered. "But wait for me a little way up." I tore some paper from my sketchbook and scribbled my address on it. "Don't come to the door," I pleaded, shaking my head.

"C'mon Steve!" someone else yelled.

"OK," he nodded. And he took the paper from me and I watched him tuck it into his pocket. "Tomorrow," he said. "About three."

He turned and I watched him go. Watched him laugh with his colleagues, watched him climb into the truck, waited for him to look back, caught his eye when he did.

Questions pounded in my head as I walked home: *What was I doing? What would people think of me? What would Papa think? What would Layla think?* But I couldn't answer myself, because I tried to convince myself it was irrelevant. Because nothing was happening. Because nothing was going to happen.

But I knew that was a lie, because something was happening, very slowly, very subtly, yet never spoken of or acknowledged.

And as I walked, I didn't see the rubbish piled at the side of the roads, didn't see the shops and schools that were falling down, didn't hear the moan of the generators, the crackle of gunfire two streets away, or feel the heat beating down on me and the dust swirling around me.

Because the hope of what tomorrow could bring had obscured the fear living in my head. If only briefly.

I kept it all from Hana, not purposefully, but it never arose in conversation; that I happened to see the same soldier every day, that we talked, that we were becoming friends, that we were going somewhere together. Not a date, of course, although I could think of no other word to give it. A meeting? An outing? In my eyes, we were just friends going out together. Weren't we?

But in the dark of the night, my worries came back. I laid in my bed, my eyes reaching through the blackness for something to rest on, but there was no light or shade. It was as if I had fallen into a hole; I could see nothing.

And I thought of those stories, stories of what happened to girls who associated with the occupiers, girls who just spoke to them, or gave a smile. Only a smile. And stories of girls selling sex to the Americans, then killed by their own families; other families forcing daughters into it, desperate for money to survive.

I heard of these girls shot, their houses burned to the ground, their families forced to leave. I knew they weren't gossip and I had added to the danger I was in, and my family, just by talking to Steve. I had made it personal.

And I thought what they would say to me, what they would do, whoever they were, these people who would know about Steve, who would know how I felt about him better than I did. I wouldn't hear their car pull up outside, their footsteps heading to my house, or their hands bang open the door. I wouldn't see their arms raise their guns or the barrel pointing at me. And I wouldn't hear the bang, I would only see the flash.

And inside me my fear grew brighter.

I sat upright in bed, my chest tight, my throat dry, fear tearing through me, my stomach turning over and over. *What had I done?*

I pulled the covers around me, longing for comfort

that no one could give, feeling sick at my own naivety and my own selfishness. *What had I been thinking? Giving him my address? Asking him to pick me up here?*

I was dismayed at my own stupidity, imagining the disbelief on Hana and Aziz's faces if I told them what I had done, what I was planning to do. The risks spiralled in my head, the dangers, the threats. I thought about Mama, taken for doing nothing wrong; I thought about Papa, killed for doing his job; and I thought about the hundreds, thousands of innocent people killed so senselessly in this war.

And what had I done? Put myself in more danger. And Hana. And Aziz. And the boys.

I wouldn't go, I vowed.

I would meet him, and would tell him I couldn't go.

Tell him I couldn't see him any more.

CHAPTER EIGHTEEN

I told Hana I felt ill. It wasn't a lie; my head pounded, my body ached, waves of nausea washed over me, and tiredness clung and dragged at me. I wanted to curl up and hide away from what I knew I had to say to Steve.

Because I didn't want to.

I felt stuck. I felt helpless.

I stayed at home, watching the clock that seemed to have slipped into slow motion. I went back to bed for a while, but couldn't sleep. I stared out of the window, depressed by what my city and my life had become, despairing of what future any of us could possibly have.

I felt angry. I felt frustrated.

I had to say no to Steve. I had to stop seeing him, stop talking to him.

At ten to three I peered out of the window, staring

down the street, but saw nobody. I tried not to pace or fidget, tried to keep my nerves hidden and not keep glancing at the clock.

It was three o'clock when I opened the door and wandered outside. I moved slowly, trying to appear casual. I stood near the gate, my eyes searching down the road. *How would he get here?* I wondered. *What would he be wearing? Not his combat uniform, surely?*

I waited, playing over in my head what I was going to say to him. Ignoring the doubt in the back of my mind, ignoring the fact that I *did* want to go with him, listening only to the part of me that was being practical, that *knew* it was too dangerous. The part of me that was reigned so totally by fear.

And I waited.

I went back in the house and out again, telling Hana I needed the fresh air, ignoring her comments about fumes and smoke, explosions and bullets. I kept my eyes low, wanting to wait, wait, and then to look up and see him there, walking towards me, smiling, welcoming, wanting to see me, to be with me. Somebody who was interested in me.

But again I looked down the road, and again he wasn't there.

It's only twenty past three, I told myself, *he's only late*. I felt so confused. What did I want? To see him? Yes, of course. Even if it was only to tell him I could never see him again, I wanted that one last time, a chance to explain, to say goodbye. I didn't want to, but I knew I had to.

And I waited.

And waited.

And with every minute that passed, I felt hope drain from me. A thousand thoughts and worries spiralled in my head. What if he'd forgotten? Lost the paper? Changed his mind? What if it was all a joke? What if he'd been killed? Blown up? Shot?

My anger grew. So much had been taken from me. So much denied. First university and now Steve. Anything that offered even the smallest glimpse of hope, the smallest hint of happiness was deemed too dangerous. I had nothing, and at that very moment, I hated everything. I felt hopeless and irrelevant, useless and pathetic. And there was nothing I could do.

If only I could go back to uni, I thought. *If only Hana would let me. Then I might have a hope at the future I want, not one she wants. I want to be independent, I want to be strong.*

I turned around, marching back in the house, heading for Hana, desperate to do something, to vent the anger inside me, direct it at someone who I felt deserved it.

"I want to go back to university," I announced.

She flicked me a look. "It's too dangerous," she said, her hands still busy scrubbing the kitchen. "You know that. There are still bombs everywhere, shootings everywhere, teachers and lecturers killed, students threatened. You want to die?"

"But you let me go out to the soldiers," I replied.

She sighed. "That's different."

"Why?" I asked.

She was silent.

"Why?" I shouted.

She stopped cleaning, rubbed her hands on a towel and moved towards me. "Because you're bringing money home," she spat. "You're earning your keep. Giving something back to us for looking after you. And maybe you'll meet someone you could marry. Take you away from here."

"You're trying to get rid of me?"

She shook her head at me. "Wake up to yourself, Lina. And take a look around you. Look at life here. What's important? An education? I don't think so. I care about you, Lina, and that's why I want to see you find someone who can look after you. Forget about university. Forget about a career. It wouldn't do you any good. It would just put you in more danger. Think about finding yourself a suitor."

I was confused, disbelieving and so, so angry. Her reasoning didn't make sense, and she knew it didn't. It was a lie. A lie because she didn't want to admit the truth even to herself. But I knew deep down why. It was Mama, all over again. Why had she been taken? Because she was educated, Hana thought, because she was clever. She didn't hide away under the protection of some man, washing pots and clothes and cooking food and bringing up babies. She had a choice. And that was all I wanted.

I couldn't follow Hana's reasoning. I didn't understand. Would Mama have been taken if she hadn't been a lawyer? Maybe not. Would Papa have been shot if he hadn't been an interpreter? Maybe not. But wasn't it more complicated than that? This war didn't follow rules. Anyone could be killed. For so many different reasons.

I wanted to scream at her, that I wasn't going to go missing like Mama, or if I did, it would be because I ran away from her. I was sick of doing as I was told, being polite, holding my tongue.

"How would you support yourself and the kids if Aziz wasn't here?" I hissed at her. "What if he was killed? What would you do? What if he crashed his taxi and couldn't drive any more? How would you feed the boys? Or a roadside bomb? What if he was dead? What if you were alone?"

She slapped me.

And I think I deserved it.

My face was hot. I was angry and humiliated, but I stood my ground, I wouldn't let her see what I was feeling.

"You're useless without him," I whispered.

I stormed from the room with tears in my eyes. And I opened the door and marched outside, the air fresh but hot, clammy on my skin.

I paced up and down, my face stinging, my chest burning, my heart thumping with rage and embarrassment. My argument with Hana had only made things worse. It had been pointless. Now there was no Steve here to make me feel better, and again there was no prospect of university. What had I been hoping for?

I looked across the city; the electricity was down again and houses hummed with the sound of generators. It drowned out my heavy breathing and my sobs. I was shocked at myself. I had never spoken to anyone like that. I felt ashamed, yet I felt relieved. I had finally said what I thought, but now wished I could take it back to save her feelings.

I felt selfish for wanting a life. I felt guilty for not being happy. I felt ungrateful for wanting more than just being alive, when so many had been killed. I was starting to hate the sound of my own moaning in my head. I needed to do something, to change the balance and to act.

Cars rumbled in the distance and in the streets around me. My pacing slowed and I stared up at the cloudless sky, the palest blue. I felt a moment's peace. Then gunfire. But now I didn't flinch. I closed my eyes, listening to the sound tear through the skies, and I knew it was coming from the east. Then I heard an explosion perhaps a mile away, screams, shouts, alarms, and I opened my eyes to see smoke lift into the air, a grey stain, growing and stretching into the sky, reminding me that I was still in Baghdad, still in a war zone.

Away in the distance I could see a US humvee and I froze. I stared at it, watching it, waiting for it to disappear, praying it wouldn't head towards me, it wouldn't stop. I knew we hadn't done anything wrong, but I knew that didn't matter. Somebody, anybody, could've nodded in our direction, for any reason, or without reason. The soldiers had the power. They could do as they pleased.

But it drove in a different direction, and as I let out the longest sigh of relief, I turned away and saw a motorbike, stopped near the end of the garden, the engine off. A man was sitting on it, a dusty jacket around him, a scarf pulled around his face, sunglasses blocking his eyes, a gun slung across his back.

His body turned around to me as if in slow motion.

I backed up, watching him, trying to think how far away I was from the house. He stretched an arm towards me, beckoning me closer, and I thought I saw his other hand move to his gun. I sucked in a breath ready to scream, but fear gripped my throat. All the horror stories I had heard, about soldiers, insurgents, militia, terrorists, flew through my head.

I forgot about my friendship with Steve.

Instead my mind and my fear showed me men, armed men, ramming into homes of Iraqis, guns pointing everywhere, at everyone; it showed me an American soldier dragging a woman into the street in her nightwear, shame dripping off her as she cried, desperate to cover herself up; it showed me a man in prison, his arms tied behind him, a lead around his neck, pulled around the room like a dog; it showed me a young woman, lying on the floor, her face bloodied, a man fastening his trousers.

Horror stories spread like wild fire. Good ones did not.

I stumbled backwards, knocking over a metal bucket, it clattered to the ground. I couldn't breathe and I felt my eyes burn with fear. Was this it? Was this my time? Was this as far as I would go? The man stared at me. I waited to become the next horror story.

"Lina," he said. "Lina, it's me."

And I breathed.

I dared to think, to believe.

The door behind me opened and Aziz stood framed by it. "What are you doing, Lina? Was that you?" he questioned.

I turned to look at him, waiting for his anger to explode because of what I had said to his wife, or for him to see the man on the bike, to question who he was, what he was doing, to think the worst, while I was hoping the best. "I was just getting some air, Uncle, I didn't see the bucket, I knocked it over. I didn't mean to disturb you."

He waved his hand around in the air. "All right, child,"

he replied. "Stay in the garden, keep safe. And no more buckets. You'll have the neighbours thinking we're being raided." He went back into the house.

I waited until the door was closed and dared to edge towards the motorbike, dared to believe that it was who I hoped it was. The man lifted off his glasses, pulled down his scarf and I saw him, I saw Steve.

"What are you doing here?" I asked.

"Lina, I'm sorry I'm late, things got difficult." He shook his head.

I tried to stop myself crying, tried so hard to hold back the sobs. I didn't want him to see me like that, to see me as weak, as someone he had to save or protect. But the tears burst from me. Was this someone who actually cared, who was showing me that he cared? He stepped forward, a hand raised in compassion, his rough fingers brushing the hair from my face, tucking it behind my ear.

My very being screamed at me to step back. My conscience shouted at me. What was I doing? What was I letting happen? Hadn't I said no to this? This friendship with the occupiers?

"Come with me," he whispered.

I stared at him. Hadn't I made my decision? Didn't I

know what I was going to say to him?

"Come with me," he repeated.

I glanced to the motorbike. "On that?"

He nodded and smiled, his face lifting me and warming me.

"I can't," I replied. But I didn't mean the words.

"Just for a couple of hours."

"But…" I searched for excuses. "What about… what will I tell them? Aziz and Hana?"

He shrugged. "You're at a neighbour's house. Playing with their children, perhaps. Or you're out selling chai. Anything."

I looked at him and I didn't care about the consequences any more. I had lived by the rules and watched my life fall apart around me. What had I done that had caused Mama to be taken and Papa to be killed? Now I was going to do something, I was going to give reason for my own demise, when before, reason seemed unnecessary.

I felt a smile spread across my face.

CHAPTER NINETEEN

Whatever happened to Sacha? Part IV

Sacha remembered the first time she saw a dead body. She remembered the shelter at Amiriyah. Her dreams and nightmares remembered it best of all. She didn't know how many bodies she watched being pulled or carried out to rest on the beige earth. Most didn't look like bodies; they looked like her mother's burnt cooking, just bigger. Lumps of meat she'd leave cooking while she glanced over notes from work. Lumps of meat she'd forget about, smoke reminding her twenty, thirty minutes later.

She remembered the evening spent in the shelter, the Eid ul-Fitr celebrations, remembered six-year-old Lina feeling sick in the early hours, remembered taking her out for air with Hana.

She closed her eyes and saw the three of them walking together, enjoying the quiet, watching the city sleep. She heard the noise of the bomb, felt it hit, heard the screams, spun around towards the noise. She saw the shock on her sister's face, her daughter's face, the smoke coming from the shelter, the second bomb hitting, people running, shrapnel flying, glass shattering.

And the smell.

They watched bodies pulled out. Some big, carried between two, some small, cradled in arms. The sound of the fire, the bombs, the screaming, was replaced with silence; heavy, waiting. Deafening. Then crying and sobbing. One person crying for a dozen.

She remembered raising her head to the sky and thanking God, she remembered her relief and thanks that Joe had been away. And she remembered her anguish, her pain, her frustration, knowing that never again would she make that journey to see her family. Not her Mama, or Papa, her grandma, or her brother or her two other sisters.

She held on to Hana and Lina as silent tears fell.

❖

Sacha looked away from her memories and down to

her hands; blistered from the spade, palms bleeding and sore, her head throbbing, the sun at its highest, its heat pouring on to the five survivors. Her tongue felt thick in her mouth, her lips cracked, her throat sticking together inside.

No water. No rest.

She looked at the bodies around her; they still looked like people; still warm as she struggled to drag a woman to her grave. She wished she could give them some dignity, wished she could pick them up in her arms and carry them to their resting places, lay them down, place a flower on their chests.

She was exhausted, weak, dehydrated. The woman's dead arm slipped away from her sweaty palm and thudded to the floor. Another survivor pulled at her feet and together they dragged her to the hole with no choice but to just push her in.

They went back for another. And another. And another.

As they back-filled the hole, Sacha didn't look at the mesh of arms and legs bent in all the wrong ways, dead eyes staring up, questioning, mouths open to scream. She turned off and shut down.

She stumbled as they were led into another yard,

barely the strength left to walk. She saw the metal ladder on the floor, saw the metal sheets on the ground, six feet across, square, with handles, punctuating the brown expanse. The sun hit them, white light reflecting back.

Her chest tightened. Fear filled her. Nausea rose in her throat.

The survivor next to her was dragged away. Ordered to lift open a lid, screaming, his hand burning on metal. Sacha watched the ladder taken to him, slid deep into the earth, disappearing. She watched the survivor climb down, the earth eating him whole, the lid clanging shut. Gone.

And there were four.

Sacha was pushed to another lid. She slid her sleeve over her hand. Lifted the lid. The smell took her back home, a hot iron left on cotton. Smoke drifting up from browned edges.

She stepped down the ladder. Heat searing through her bare feet. Darkness engulfed her. The square of light she was leaving behind retracting. The ladder was pulled away. Darkness swallowed her, absorbed her.

The lid clanged shut and there was nothing.

Nothing but darkness and heat and smell.

She collapsed to the ground.

…She dreamed. Christmas. A tree inside, huge, stretching to the ceiling. On top, an angel, blonde hair, golden wings. Presents underneath. Small fingers flicking at gift tags. One for Hana, for Evan, for Samara, for Fay. One for Sacha. Her sisters. Her brother. A hum of conversation, laughter, happiness. The smell of food, drifting, floating. A full household, friends, relatives, neighbours, colleagues. Warmth, humanity, kindness…

…Music blares, bright, raucous. Neon lights, laughter and shrieking. A rollercoaster thunders towards the ground. A pirate ship swings back and forth. Her papa takes her hand, pulls her to the ghost ride. Her face whitens and he laughs, tussling her hair, holding her in his arms, protecting her. She feels his warmth, feels his laughter vibrate in his chest…

…A black dress, a man sits next to her. A large hall. She watches the orchestra, she feels the music, hears the music. Never forgetting the man sitting next to her. She closes her eyes, listens to Gershwin, Mozart, Beethoven. She listens to the breathing of the man next to her…

She wakes back into the darkness. The smell of what she doesn't want to imagine turns her stomach. She blinks, her eyes focusing, adjusting to the dark, shapes swirl before her.

"Don't be frightened," says a voice. "I won't hurt you."

Sacha could make out the shape of a person in front of her. The faintest needle of light squeezing between the side of the metal lid metres above her head. The voice stepped forward. The light too small to illuminate much, her image pieced together, a searchlight scanning indiscriminately and infinitesimally.

Sacha's sanity rested on a knife edge and she felt herself swaying.

"I've been here a long time," the voice continued. "My name is Nahla. The man over there is Salam."

Sacha waited to hear Salam introduce himself, but silence remained. She searched the darkness for Nahla.

"It'll be nice to have company again," Nahla continued. "Someone to talk to when I'm dying. As Salam talked to me."

Sacha frowned. She wanted to wake up. *Could my imagination conjure this hell?* she thought. She sniffed again and retched.

"He's dead?" she asked.

"About a week ago," Nahla replied. "They won't take him. I moved him over to the corner, but I can't do any more. He was heavy, too heavy for me. It took me days to get him that far. When I die, you can lay me next to him."

"I need to sit down," Sacha said.

Nahla put her hand on Sacha's shoulder and led her to the wall. They sat together. As she steadied her breathing her wide eyes searched around, but the edges, the walls, blurred away, the size, the space, impossible to fathom. In one corner she could make out the dead man, next to him a bucket, dark splodges around it.

"The bucket is never emptied," Nahla told her. "I put Salam next to it to keep the smell together."

Sacha's head shook.

"They won't let you out for the toilet. They probably won't let you out ever again. You'll die in here."

Sacha felt Nahla lean in close, her eyes needling through the dark. "Judging by the look of you, you'll die before me. Not in good shape, are you? Been in prison?"

Sacha nodded.

Her thoughts spun back to her dream. She remembered the necklace, shining in her imagination like a beacon of love and comfort. A reminder of her husband, her child. She reached into her jacket. A tiny zipped pocket. She remembered buying the suit, frowning at the pocket, wondering why on earth it was there. She remembered that day, in her office, all that time ago. She remembered walking into the foyer at work, pausing, seeing the men outside waiting for her, then reaching up, unclipping her necklace and dropping it into her pocket, wanting and hoping to keep it with her and keep it safe.

All this time, she thought, *and it's still here.*

She pulled the necklace out, the chain pressing into her fingers as she clung on to it. She held it to her face. The cold, the smoothness of the stone against her lips. She ran her thumb across it and remembered her family.

CHAPTER TWENTY

I was on the back of the motorbike, a pair of old trousers on, a scarf around my face and head, sunglasses hiding my eyes. Could anyone tell it was me? That I was female? That I was with a soldier?

I hoped not.

I waited for him to start the engine, for it to roar into life and I felt nervous, worried, yet exhilarated. *What should I do with my hands?* I thought. *Where do I put them? How do I stay on?* I felt embarrassed at the thought of holding on to his waist, or putting my arms around him or of being that close to him.

But as we moved off, my hands went straight to him, clinging to him as the bike leaned in and out of corners, dodged around pedestrians and squeezed between cars. I sheltered behind him, my face tucked into him, and my eyes closed. I felt the acceleration pull at my stomach and the air blowing at my clothes, and I was transported away.

And I became braver. After he'd dodged through roadblocks and passed through checkpoints with a nod and a word to the right person, I lifted my head more, and I kept my eyes open, and I watched the city fly past me.

We left behind the houses, the bustling streets and busy roads, the shells of burnt-out cars and remnants of homes, the children on street corners who had lost mothers and the men strolling around who had lost jobs.

And I left behind my fears and my worries, my grief and frustrations.

We turned on to an old track and I pulled the scarf from my head, the wind lifting through my hair, buffeting at my face and around my clothes. It took away my breath as I shouted up to the sky, and for a moment I lifted up my arms, trailing the scarf behind me and stretching out my fingertips.

The breeze was warm, the air was clear and the track in front of us was empty.

I felt alive. I felt free. And I was – for those brief few moments, I was free.

When we stopped I didn't know where we were, yet I didn't particularly care. I didn't know how long we had travelled for, but to me it felt like another world, a world beyond the city. A lake stretched out in front of us, the water blue and clear, a dusty path leading around it, long grasses stretching up here and there.

The engine was off and I could hear nothing.

We stood without saying a word, staring across the lake and away into the distance.

He beckoned me to follow him as he moved towards the water's edge. Still neither of us spoke, and I could hear now the rustle of the grasses under my feet and against my legs, the brush of his jacket as he walked, the faint creak of my shoes.

I followed him. And we sat down together. And in the August heat and in silence, we watched the ripple of the water, the swaying of the grass, a flock of birds swoop low then lift up and away.

"It's so quiet," I whispered.

He nodded. "No generators. No traffic."

"No gunfire," I said. I closed my eyes and I felt the stillness, the calm and the peace. I felt it wash over me. I listened to nothing but the lightness of the silence. "It's beautiful," I said, my eyes still closed.

I felt the tension drift from my shoulders, my head clear of stress, my whole body ease and loosen. My skin was warm, the air was clear and the company was good. Fear seemed distant.

I opened my eyes again and thought. I pulled my bag towards me, flicking it open and pulling out my sketchbook. "I want to show you something," I said. Steve shuffled towards me as I opened the pages. "I drew these the month before the war began, February 2003. I wanted to try to remember the city how it was, before anything happened."

I turned the page. "That's Firdos Square," I said. "Paradise Square, you call it. Not a square at all. A roundabout, really. Saddam's statue in the middle before it was pulled down. See how big it was? It used to stare at you as you drove up the road towards it." I pointed to the next one. "A street not far from where I lived. You see the houses there?" I tapped my finger on a row of white houses edged with small, concrete walls. "They were completely destroyed. That line of palm trees? They were burnt down."

He didn't say a word.

I turned another page. "This," I said, "I drew when I was sitting at the bank of the river with some friends. That tall building in the background is the old communications tower. It was a landmark, before the sides of it were ripped out." I stared at it for a moment, remembering drawing its straight lines, its angular walls, and its arched windows.

"This one is Ramadan Mosque, but it's not very good, because you can't get any idea of the colour. It's beautiful; turquoise, and deep blue patterns with orange and white and a lovely green. I only have my pencil," I said.

He scanned over the rest of my drawings without saying a word. A church with its cross stretching into the cloudless sky, the low Sarafiya bridge with its heavy iron spreading along it like a cage, Baghdad museum standing magnificent with its two square towers as if it was a fortress protecting its treasures inside.

"It's wonderful," he said at last. "You never said, y'know, that you can draw."

I smiled at him. I didn't want to share with him my dream of becoming an architect. It seemed so hopeless at that moment, a senseless dream that could never come true.

"You should draw this," he said, nodding out to the lake.

And in the sunshine, with only birdsong breaking the quiet, I took my pencil and sketched the lake, the water shimmering, the grasses paused as they swayed, the skyline of Baghdad hiding in the distance.

And when he wasn't looking, I turned the page and I sketched Steve, my pencil dancing through his short, blonde hair; stuttering along his stubbled chin; gliding up his high cheekbones and around his mouth. I sketched his T-shirt bagging at his neck, his shoulder blades visible through the material, and the line of his arm as it stretched out and rested on his knee. I wished I was better at drawing.

I flicked back to my sketch of the lake. "How did you know about this place?" I asked.

"A friend told me," he replied. "I'm glad you agreed to come."

I paused. "I wasn't going to. I was going to tell you then that I couldn't go, couldn't see you again."

He frowned at me.

I sighed and looked away. "It's so difficult," I said. "So dangerous. I don't know what would happen if people knew I was here with you."

He nodded.

"I don't know what I think about all this. You confuse

me. I don't want you to be an American. Don't want you to be a soldier. Don't need you to come into my life and rescue me."

"I'm not…"

"But you are. However little. Not physically, but you lift me, lift my spirits, my thoughts, away from what I'm living in, the hell that surrounds me and threatens me every day." I couldn't believe what I was saying, couldn't believe the honesty in my words. "You, just you, being with you, thinking of you, can pause that fear that I live in, the thought that I'm not going to make it to tomorrow, even if it's only for two minutes, it's two minutes that make me feel awake again, alive and… and hopeful that there is more. That maybe, maybe one day, things *will* get better."

"But that's a good thing, isn't it? That I can do that for you? Or is that not enough?"

I shook my head. "It shouldn't be like that," I whispered. "I shouldn't need you to make me feel better."

I glanced away into the distance, back towards Baghdad.

"Do you wish we were gone?" he asked. "The soldiers? Do you think it would be better?"

I looked up at him, a fragment of light reflecting in

his blue eyes. "I don't know," I said. "Not you. I don't want you to go. But… I don't know what the answer is. I don't think anyone does. Not really. Everyone thinks they do but…" My voice trailed away. Hadn't every single Iraqi, whether Sunni, Shia, Christian, Kurd or whatever religion or faith, thought about all these questions, and thought they knew the answer only to change their minds a few days or weeks later? What about the Americans? The British? Did they have any answers for us? Did they know what to do?

"It's a mess," I said, shrugging. I didn't want to talk about it with him, not of what my country had become, not of the forces, the militia that it now housed, the insurgents, Al-Qaeda, not of our daily struggle for survival. Not here. Not now.

I felt him sigh, and he turned to me. "Why don't you leave?" he whispered. I spun around to him, a lurch in my stomach, my breath caught.

"Leave?" I repeated.

He nodded. "Leave the country. Go somewhere safer. I could help you. I could find out. Question people. See how you could do it. Where you could go."

And I stopped and thought. But it seemed unbelievable and impossible. How could I leave without finding out about Mama? But then…? What had Papa told me, all that time ago? To leave if things became too bad, if something happened to him… And I dared to think about it.

"At least let me find out for you," he said.

"Why?" I asked, shaking my head. "Why would you do that for me?"

"Lina," he sighed. "Y'know, I'm sorry. For everything. For your country, for your friends, for your papa, for all this destruction." He lowered his voice. "But it's not my doing. And I'm not trying to rescue you, or save you, and I'd like to keep you here, just to be with you, and to know what was happening with you. But that's selfish. I want you to be safe."

His words surprised me. Shocked me. They lifted me and made my spirits dare to believe that to someone, I mattered. That someone cared. With Papa gone, with Mama missing, I felt alone. I was special to no one. I was no one's priority. Yet this? I wanted to believe I was special to him. I looked at him. Was I imagining the warmth and compassion I thought I could see?

I wanted to believe it. I wanted it to be real. But my thoughts and worries kept coming back to that one thing over and over again. "But," I whispered, "you're

American. And you're a soldier."

He laughed. "Yeah, I am. But so what? You're Iraqi." He shrugged. "Y'know, I would get into so much trouble if people found out I was here too, but I don't care. I'm not going to worry about it. I don't know when we're going to see each other again. So, let's forget about it for now. While we're here, away from everything. Forget I'm American and forget I'm a soldier. And I'll forget you're Iraqi. And we'll just be who we are, with no labels. OK?"

Yes, I thought to myself. *Yes*.

"I'm Steve," he said, stretching out his hand towards me. "Pleased to meet you."

"Lina," I whispered. I placed my hand in his, and we shook.

But he didn't let go. And I didn't pull away.

And in the quiet and calm, for an hour that felt like only five minutes, we whispered about things that were a million miles away from the despair and fear that waited for us both.

And in the back of my mind, I thought about leaving.

CHAPTER TWENTY-ONE

He said it again as I reached home, as I handed back the scarf and the glasses, and as I looked around for somewhere to change out of the trousers once he had left. "I don't know when I can see you again," he said. "But I'll try."

I believed him.

And before he could ride away, before we could be seen, I pulled my sketchbook from my bag and tore out my drawing of the lake. I handed it to him, my name scrawled in the corner, the year, 2004, written next to it. "Keep it," I said.

He stared at it for a moment. "Thank you," he whispered at last. Then he rolled it up and hid it inside his jacket. "I'll look after it."

And as he said goodbye to me with just a look, but a

look that meant so much, my decision was forming in my head. Whether it was that time spent with Steve, that I knew may never happen again, or the argument with Hana before, or the explosions and gunfire that sounded out across the city again. Or the twenty minutes we had that evening with electricity where we watched news of yet another suicide bomb, yet more bloodied children, and yet more crying mothers. Or Aziz returning home late with yet more stories of roadblocks and street closures, trigger-happy soldiers that looked like school children.

I was becoming numb to it.

Life was passing me by in dream.

And that hour I'd spent with Steve had reminded me so much of what I, what we all, were missing. It reminded me of living.

I decided I was leaving.

I would get the money. I would talk to people. I would find out how to get out of the country. I didn't know where to start, where to head for. Would Syria still let Iraqis in? If not, where else? Iran wasn't an option, Turkey meant heading north through the mountains, countless checkpoints and no doubt terrorists. Kuwait? Saudi Arabia? How would I find out? Who should I talk to? If I was a refugee would I be allowed to work? To study? What rights would I have? Where would I live? I hoped Steve would find out for me.

A million questions whirred in my head, and while doubt still flowed, and while the guilt of leaving Mama, not finding out about her, lingered, it all led back to the certainty that I must leave. That if I did not, I would eventually be killed, or I would go insane. That I would lose my life one way or another.

✣

Weeks passed and I waited and hoped to see Steve again. The thought of him stayed in my head, although I tried so hard for it not to. *Does he still have my address?* I wondered. *Will he turn up one day? Will he come back to the gas station? Will I see him on patrol?*

There were no knocks at the door or rumours or stories about me, for now at least, and for that I was grateful. Still, every day I would go out selling chai, wishing he would be there, trying to stop the hope inside me, trying to tell myself it was futile. I wanted to ask the other soldiers, but daren't, and so many had changed there seemed little chance that they knew him.

I had been given the smallest glimpse of something

that felt like happiness only to feel it being pulled away from me.

I felt lonely.

I was tired of the war, the occupation. I doubted if peace would ever find us, and I doubted still further that Mama would ever return. I could feel the threat of acceptance that she was dead. I was at a loss what to do.

Again, I thought about the money. I thought about leaving the country, beginning afresh somewhere else. But what future would I have? What about when the money ran out? What could I do? And I remembered Papa, how he waited and waited for Mama. Would he want me to do the same?

I felt autumn approaching, the change in the air, the chance of rain and in the distance another Christmas threatened far too quickly. It stuck in my head like a reminder of everything that had passed. It would be the second Christmas without Papa. Sixth without Mama. Two since that trepidation rose in me like fire as war approached. Tanks tearing through our city, soldiers marching through my home; I thought by now we would be at peace, or at least on our way towards it, but if anything it seemed further away. Now there was lawlessness.

I heard of so many people leaving. A family who had come home to a noose hanging from a light fitting, a photo of their daughter taped inside it. What had she done? A woman who found a death threat wrapped around a bullet on her doorstep. A couple whose shop was bombed by insurgents who then threatened to kill them both.

And stories of torture; men and women and children abducted, their fingernails removed, or their teeth or eyelids; holes drilled in their bodies with power tools. How could anyone protect themselves when everyone was someone else's enemy? Be they Sunni or Shia, Christian or Arab. If you were gay, if you sold alcohol, if you didn't cover your head, if you danced.

I was living a horror film with no end credits in sight. But this wasn't a film, or a dream, or a story. This was life. And I couldn't just press the off button, or wake up, or slam the pages shut.

I had to live it.

But I couldn't any longer.

CHAPTER TWENTY-TWO

Christmas came around again too soon.

Aziz and Hana usually decorated their house with lights, as me and Papa had done ours, outside and in, a plastic tree sparkling in the corner, presents underneath. But this year as with the last there was nothing. How could we? With electricity intermittent and erratic, we daren't use it on Christmas lights. And we couldn't risk advertising our religion with a smiling Santa and a swaddled baby Jesus. And midnight mass? I doubt even the vicar would make it there alive.

It was glum. The excitement was lost.

Then, as I stared across the room, the candlelight flickering on the boys' faces, there was the tiniest knock on the door.

The very air in the room seemed to freeze.

We stopped still in time, waiting, dread and fear seeping in through every gap; under doors, through windows, from behind cupboards and around corners. I looked up, as did we all, and all eyes rested on Aziz. None of us breathed, and it seemed a mist of fear was spreading out across the floor, growing around our ankles, pulling up our legs, holding us motionless and useless, while every sound but the droning of the generators stopped. Aziz's brow furrowed and he exhaled as if trying to blow his worries away from him.

"Stay where you are," he whispered as he stood up. But we didn't need telling.

I knew most houses kept a gun for protection, an AK-47 usually, and often the boys in the house were taught how to use it, how to defend themselves and their families, but I didn't think Aziz would own one. I couldn't imagine one in the hands of a man so mild, so peace-loving, so friendly; couldn't imagine him pointing it at anyone, looking down the sights, shooting.

But what if someone broke in, if troops came searching for someone, something, as they often did, or militia, or burglars even? Our imaginations conjured up images of soldiers, insurgents, faceless, nameless enemies who had finally come for us.

What if someone saw me with Steve?

What if someone had come to punish me?

Then Aziz came back into the room with an AK-47 in his hands and I felt my mouth fall open with shock. The eldest boy followed him, passing him a loaded magazine, and across the silence I heard grinding, the sickening noise as he prepared the gun. The whole scene in front of me was so wrong. What had this war turned my family into?

And it hit me, what was happening to our country and our lives, that Aziz *could* kill someone, *could* squeeze that trigger and send that bullet out, and actually cause someone's death. Because I knew he would, if he needed to. For his family, for himself.

Had we all turned into killers?

The knock sounded again, and with a brief look back, with fear so visible in his eyes, his family's safety seeming to drag and pull at him, slowing him down, I watched him walk towards the door.

I thought back to the bombing, back to the day Papa died, the knock on the door, that terrible, terrible feeling inside, knowing I couldn't escape whatever looked for me.

And we waited. For what seemed an eternity. For

shouts or screams, gunfire or explosions.

My eyes closed, my ears craned through the silence. What was that I could hear? Aziz's voice. And another. Female. Quiet. Soft. I felt my body relax, felt my face smooth and my eyes open, and there in front of me was Layla.

"You gave us a fright," said Aziz, strolling away, the gun uncomfortable in his hands.

And although I felt relief fill me, it brought with it fear and dread that something had happened to her family. Why else would she be here? But I looked into her eyes, and I could see the love of my friend smiling back at me.

❖

We sat together in my room and as she tried to explain and apologise, and as I tried to understand, the awkwardness that had been between us for nearly two years lifted.

For half an hour we laughed and chatted like schoolgirls, and I felt the worry and anxiety lift from me with each smile and each giggle. We touched on nothing serious, not a word of war or politics, or the lack of food and water and electricity. I didn't mention how much I missed uni, even with the haphazard classes, and the worrying journey there, and the phone calls made to loved ones on your arrival every day.

And we didn't mention Papa.

After that half an hour, she stood to leave and pulled something from her pocket.

"Merry Christmas," she said, and I felt pinpricks on my skin, and my eyes well with tears. She placed a small package in my hands, wrapped in yesterday's newspaper.

Gently I pulled at the newspaper that would normally bring nothing but gloom, and stared down at the postcard in a tattered wooden frame in my hand. It was beautiful.

"Where did you get this?" I asked, marvelling at the gift.

She was beaming now. "I was lucky," she replied.

I traced my finger along the postcard of St Paul's Cathedral in London. She knew this was one of my favourite buildings, a place I'd love to go, but knew I never would, or could. I was mesmerised by it. I remembered Papa's story of it – his visit there with Mama. And I marvelled over how special something so far away could feel, how it could hold so many feelings for me, so many memories, of Papa, of Mama, their time in London, their love for each other, and that special time I had with Papa as he shared his memories with me.

I love Iraqi architecture too: the turquoise of the Martyrs Monument, the strangeness of its fat teardrop shape; the ancient walls of Babylon, crumbling away in places but still the raised outline of the God of Marduk visible in the stonework; the beauty and colour of the Ramadan Mosque, the minute tiles, blues and greens and purples, reflecting the sunlight, its elaborateness contrasting the dark abayas, the dishdashas of those entering it.

Those buildings are why I wanted to be an architect.

I had seen so much destroyed in my city, to be part of it being built back up again would be a dream. And although some days I felt desperate to leave Iraq so I could study and learn, travel and see new things – visit Paris, climb the Eiffel Tower; see the Spanish Steps in Rome; Gaudi's cathedral in Barcelona; the Acropolis in Athens; Red Square in Moscow – that had been replaced by an urgent need to leave Iraq purely to survive.

I looked up to Layla, stunned by the thoughtfulness of this gift, yet its simplicity. It was the kind of gift it is only possible to receive from a friend who truly knows and loves you. I moved forward and hugged her, and we held each other tight for so long that all those months of not speaking, of avoiding each other, melted away.

"I wish I'd got you something," I muttered into her hair.

I felt her shake her head. She moved away and looked at me. "Christmas isn't for me," she replied. She sighed and turned away. "I have to go," she said. "My family are visiting someone close by, I promised I wouldn't be long." And as I walked back through the house with her, as we reached the door, we paused.

"I miss being your friend," she said.

I watched the tears slipping down her face, took her hand and kissed it. "We'll always be friends," I replied, and I hoped it was true.

And I watched from the door as Aziz escorted her back to her family, to the friends they were visiting. As they moved further away, they became silhouettes, the sun setting in front of them and I only knew who the shapes were because my eyes had followed them.

The day was drawing in. The sky was darkening, edged with deep red and oranges and purple hues. I wished I could lose myself in it.

Because above me it was peaceful.

Above me it was beautiful.

And I wished I could fly up there. If only for a few minutes.

As I sat back down in my room, the postcard next to me on the bed, I felt guilt claw at me. *I should feel happy,* I thought. *My friend, my best friend, has visited me, has been so thoughtful as to bring me a wonderful gift.*

But I didn't. Instead I felt all I had lost. Felt it heavy on my shoulders. And I felt angry. I wanted to be back in my house, with my papa, with Layla across the road from me, with university to go to, with friends to visit, places to go to in safety. With a life to live.

As we tried to celebrate Christmas, I realised how few Christians were left in the city. I mentioned it to Aziz and his response was brief: "We are rats leaving a sinking ship."

I did not wish to be the only rat left.

CHAPTER TWENTY-THREE

Whatever happened to Sacha? Part V

How much time passed in the dark, in the hole, in the ground, she had no idea. Daylight was barely distinguishable, and the hours passed like days, months or years, as her thoughts and memories spiralled out of control.

And although on the first day she waited for the lid to open, for her name to be shouted and to be taken out and tortured or killed, it didn't happen, and gradually she let herself feel some semblance of relief, a sense of peace and gratitude at being left alone. No torture or electricity, no whips or chains, no sounds of women crying or screaming or sobbing. No guard at the door hollering her name, no walk down to that room with fear in her belly like a sickness.

And on that day, that first day, Sacha stepped away from reality, retreating into her head and her memories. Thoughts of her husband and her daughter filled her hours, memories of her mother and father, her sisters and brother, her days at school, studying in London, trips to the orchestra, exams, first house, first day at work, first case in court. Markers of her life.

One by one she lifted each memory out of its box, replayed it in her mind, watching it unfold before her like an old film, before wrapping it up again and tucking it back inside.

And the hours passed. And the days. And the weeks.

And sometimes the lid would open, their eyes would close against the sunlight glaring down, trying to catch the dried bread dropped in, waiting as the bucket of water was lowered down on a length of rope, her and Nahla standing underneath, grateful for any splash upon their faces, their mouths wide, their tongues out, catching drips like dancing snowflakes.

But the heat inside baked them; the stench swirling and writhing around them, hope evading them, desperation clawing at them.

While she sat in the dark, the question came to her

often: if she wanted death to release her. *Is wanting, or praying for death, the same as suicide?* she thought. *Is it a sin? God gives us life, should I be wishing it away? But what god does this, allows this? Do I deserve this?*

And with those questions, came doubts in the belief she had carried since childhood, the religion she was born into. Yet the thought of losing her faith scared her more than death. While she believed, she knew that heaven waited for her, that she would, in time, be reunited with her family. Her mother and father would smile at her again, her husband would kiss her again, and she would again hold her daughter to her.

Fear kept her belief singing in her chest.

Fear stopped her doubting.

Fear held her god up high and the gates wide open for her arrival.

CHAPTER TWENTY-FOUR

I clung to the memory of that day with Steve. And I wished for the chance to meet properly again, where we could pretend he wasn't a soldier, where we could be ourselves, and my head dreamed of scenarios where impossible things do happen.

And time ticked on. The weeks and months disappearing behind me. My life disappearing while I waited; to see Steve, to decide if I should leave Iraq, to find the courage to go.

But the question of Mama never left my head and when I thought about leaving, I felt heavy with guilt. I should stay. I should wait for her. I should never give up on her. Never.

I would look at that photo, of Mama and Papa holding me as a baby, the smiles on their faces, the green necklace around Mama's neck, the flash from the camera glinting from it and I would ask myself what I thought she would want me to do. To stay here? To wait for her? I couldn't answer. I would return, I told myself. When things were better, safer. And I would find her when it was safe to travel around the city, when the prisons were fair places.

Was I convincing myself?

I started to hate the sound of my own thoughts; whining, moaning, negative. I wanted to smile and laugh, tell stories of good news. But I didn't know of any.

But as another new year approached, when Aziz had to queue with five hundred other cars for over thirteen hours to fill up, when we had no electricity for three days, no fuel for the generators so we could cook, when things were so bad, after another night kept awake by explosions and gunfire, another day arriving home in tears because of what I'd seen on the way, I knew it was time for me to leave. I knew there was no choice for me any more.

It was New Year's Eve. Another one. I longed for some time alone, some quiet, some peace to clear my head, to think about the past year, to remember Papa. And I convinced Hana to let me out of the house alone.

Only for ten minutes, I told her, I promised her.

But of course there was no quiet or peace. The streets were as dangerous as ever, and thinking I could walk around without worrying about every street corner or window or approaching car was naive.

I strolled down streets with my head down, listening to sounds around me. The grumble of a car engine, the putting of a moped, Arabic chatter here and there.

And the shout of a soldier.

I looked up, a trooper on the other side of the road, his gait so familiar to me, the way he held his rifle. My eyes stopped, blurring away what surrounded me, and focused upon him. I crossed the road, watching him. Daring to believe that it was him. And he turned and saw me, smiling as if it was only yesterday we had been to the lake.

For a moment we stood next to each other, awkward, not knowing what to say, what to do. I wanted to stretch out a hand to him, or for him to put an arm around me and hold me, but I knew that couldn't happen, that something so simple, so natural, was impossible. But it was there, that feeling, that acknowledgement of something, as we stood together with a smile, and as we turned together and walked.

"You still thinking of leaving?" he asked.

I sighed. *Was I?* I asked myself. And I nodded.

"You want to go to Europe?" he said, a vague smile on his face. "Think I know of someone who can get you there."

"Europe?" I questioned, nerves leaping at my throat. "That's a long way."

"But you'd be safe."

I didn't know what to say. Not since before Papa died had I imagined going as far away as Europe. "I was thinking of somewhere closer. Syria or Jordan. Then when things are better…"

He let out a sigh. "You want to come back?"

"It's my home," I replied. "Everything I know is here… I don't know if… if I would dare go anywhere else."

He shrugged his shoulders. "Lina, I've talked to people, they say you're not allowed to work in Syria, they say people have to return here when their money's gone. That they're no better off. You'd have to support yourself. Could you do that? Your aunt's not going to send money, is she? They said about people being turned away at borders and having to live in tents, or in refugee camps." He stopped walking and stared at me. "I wish I could take you home with me. Back to the States. Get you a place to live. A job, or hell, into college." He sighed. "That's not gonna happen. But you can get to Europe."

We both fell silent. I felt somehow disappointed. Had I really been hoping for him to take me with him? To America? Is that what I secretly wanted? Did he mean that much to me or was he just someone who had shown me some compassion? I didn't know now. I was so scared. Scared to go, scared to stay. What should I do? I had the money from Papa; that would support me for a long time in Syria. But would it be for long enough?

"You said you had money, right?" Steve asked.

I nodded, thinking of the box in the wall in my old house.

"Then it's not a problem. Believe me. This guy, he'll take you in a truck from here, through Syria, then to Greece, Italy, and if you want, France and England."

My head reeled. "England?" I thought of Papa's friends there. Maybe they could help me. "And a passport?"

"Yeah. A British passport. Then, y'know, you can get set up over there. Hell, I could even come over to see you. Or you could come to me."

I struggled to think straight. It seemed like fantasy, a dream, the opportunity of a new life, in a new country. A safe country? With a passport?

"Is it…? It's not legal, is it?"

He smiled at me with his blue eyes.

"How much?" I asked.

We walked together, my head covered, my body covered, my face low, I was anonymous to anyone but him. And I didn't even think what it must look like; an Iraqi girl walking down the street with an American soldier. Embroiled in a serious conversation. I didn't notice what street we were on, who we walked past, or even if anyone stared or shouted comments at us. My head was trapped in a mixture of excitement at the possibilities Steve was offering me, and the fear of what it would actually mean. All the places I would pass on the way. A new country to live in, to explore. All the things to see when I got there. The unknown. To travel all that way. A stowaway in a truck or boat. At the mercy of a stranger. And what about returning for Mama?

"Nine thousand dollars," he replied.

I didn't repeat it. I didn't stop walking.

"I wish I could offer you some, but…"

I shook my head. "I wouldn't take it from you," I replied.

"Hell, you would. I'd make sure you would. I'd pay the whole damn thing if I could, to know you'd be safe…"

I shook my head. "I can do it."

We walked on in silence and thought. Nine thousand dollars. I thought of the money, hidden in a tin, behind the broken brick, at the top of the wall, at the bottom of the stairs, in the basement. There was fifteen thousand in there. That would leave me some spare. I'd have some to live off when I got there. Or I could leave some for Hana and Aziz. Or I could do both.

"What about when I get there?" I asked. "What about work, or somewhere to live?"

"Yeah, this guy, who I was talking to, said he'll help you, get you some work, somewhere to sleep until you're sorted." He turned to me, staring at me with such seriousness. "You want to go?"

I paused. I felt excited, scared, hopeful, worried. My head whirred from one decision to another, a thousand questions in my head, a thousand scenarios playing out in my imagination. What would the journey be like? Would it be safe? Would I be caught? What would life be like when I got there? What would I do? How would I live? Would I be happy?

I didn't understand why Steve was doing this for me. A stranger in my land and my life, and yet he cared about me enough to help me.

"When does the truck leave?" I asked.

"Three days," he replied.

"Three days?" I repeated quietly. My stomach turned upside down; I felt sick. My thoughts spun. Three days. Three sleeps. Three more mornings checking I was still alive. Could I really do this?

We turned the corner at the end of the street, and I saw the rest of his squad.

"I have to go." He took a piece of paper from his pocket. "This is where you need to be, near the Grand Mosque," he said. "And the time. You give the money to the driver. And there's my email address. When you get to England, get in touch."

"Will I see you before I go?"

"I don't know."

I nodded and we paused, awkward. His hand lifted to my face, but withdrew. "I'm glad we met," he whispered, "but I wish it had been different. Wish we could've met somewhere else." He sighed and lowered his head. He took a step towards me. "When this is all over we'll meet somewhere else, some *time* else, and it'll be different. Maybe you'll be in England, in London. And you'll be standing looking at Buckingham Palace. It'll be raining, because it always does in London. And a red bus will pull p off. Neither of us will have an umbrella,

timistic, and we were expecting sun. I'll

standing near the railings, with beautiful

n her back, and I'll walk towards her,

n around with your deep brown eyes and

s handsome blond-haired, blue-eyed man

u."

me?" I said. I pretended to appraise him, my

to one side. "Passable, maybe. But handsome?"

ghed. "You'll smile back at me, the rain pouring

our face. We'll say something like, 'Haven't we

fore? You seem familiar?' and we'll laugh. I'll lift

my arms, tears mixing with rain on our faces."

"I would like that," I said, quietly. "I would like to meet you in London."

He placed the paper in my palm and held my hand. Just for a moment. And I couldn't say a word. I could only stare at him.

"Some day," he whispered. "Some time."

And he lifted his hand to my face again, and I felt his fingers touch my cheek and wipe away a tear.

And with the vaguest of smiles, he turned and walked away.

CHAPTER TWENTY-FIVE

I walked home with a strange feeling in my chest.

England, I thought.

But what about...? And my head swam with all the *what abouts?* What about Mama, wherever she may be? What about Hana and Aziz? What about Layla? What about all my other friends?

Memories hung around me like flies. They played out in my mind like a film. I could see Mama kissing me goodbye on my first day of school; I could see myself carried on Papa's shoulders through a market bustling with people, smells and chatter coming from everywhere; I could see the three of us sat at home, laughing at the television. I could see ordinary, everyday memories. Family memories. But of a family that no longer existed.

I cried for what my country, my city, had suffered. I

cried for what its people had endured. I cried for the missing, the injured, the dead. For Mama. For Papa. I cried for the living. I cried for us all.

But this was the right thing to do, and I knew that it was. I loved my country, I loved my home, but right then, at that time, it wasn't the right place for me to be. I would return, I vowed I would. And I would return educated, with my profession, an architect, and with it, I would help rebuild my beloved country to what it once was. Better than it was.

But until then, until I returned, I would carry the memories it had given me.

And the air seemed lighter as I walked, and the heat less suffocating, and the thought of going back to Hana and Aziz's house and their awful children didn't fill me with dread, because that wasn't where my future waited for me.

Three days and I would be on my way to a new life.

✣

I arrived back to a house full of friends, relatives and neighbours. New Year's Eve, I reminded myself. I strolled into the kitchen to find Hana preparing food, other women with her, and their chatter was beautiful.

Smells of kebabs, bread and popcorn for the children flowed through the house, and compassion, laughter and friendship filled the air. It was comforting. It was uplifting and I let it flow over me. For one evening, it seemed, troubles were put aside. Our different religions were never mentioned, nor how this meeting may be viewed by our fellow Iraqis, or even how the Americans may think of us as a terrorist cell.

The absurdity of it all.

We didn't care. Or at least, we pretended not to.

The evening drew on, it became later and later. I watched Hana, seeing her look to the clock every few minutes, check the watch at her wrist, look out of the window, to the door. And I realised Aziz was not yet home.

As she returned to the kitchen, I followed her.

"He should be back by now," she whispered, her head kept low, her eyes away from mine.

I could see the worry on her face. "Well," I began, "maybe with it being New Year's Eve, there's more business."

She didn't reply.

"Or roadblocks. Maybe there are more roadblocks and it's slowed him down."

Still she was silent.

"Or maybe the car's broken down."

She spun round and stared at me. "Or maybe he's dead," she spat.

I had no reply for that.

Maybe he *was* dead.

✤

The minutes seeped by. Worry and uncertainty spread through the house as happiness seeped from it. I watched Hana's fear grow. She paced the house, tidied pots and pans away, continually offered drinks to guests. Her body was busy with errands, her mind busy with worry. Her eyes flicked to the clock, to the door, to the window, to the phone. She paused at every noise, her eyes narrowed as her ears stretched across the house, searching for what she had heard, testing to see if it was her husband in his car.

Still he was not home.

Three hours passed. New Year ticked ever closer. Was this how we would remember it? "Remember New Year's Eve 2004?" we would say. "Oh, yes, that was when Aziz didn't come home." Like everything else since this war began. How did you remember things? Time could be slow, a day feeling like a year, chaotic; dates became meaningless. Instead, events stood out like statues, or bookmarks of time. *When did I last see Rafa from school?* I would think, searching my head for a date, yet when none came, I would remember, *the day the mosque in Samarra was bombed. What about your neighbour Salam? Hmm, the day of all the suicide bombs, the ambulance blown up at the Red Cross.*

Most people left, going home with worried faces, words of reassurance uttered, although knowingly helpless. Our neighbours, Saad and Fatima, stayed, and while they sat with Hana as she wrung her hands and wiped her brow and held back tears, I put the boys to bed, comforting them with ideas that their Papa was working late.

Midnight loomed. We phoned his work colleagues, places he may have picked up a fare, friends he may have gone to visit, but nobody had seen him since six o'clock. Panic rose in me, uselessness, fear of what we would discover, what had become of him. And despite the danger, the roadblocks, the possible bombs, the very real threat of death, Saad and his grown-up son, Jamail, drove out to search for him. And Hana and Fatima and myself, and the boys pretending to sleep, waited.

And waited.

There is nothing worse, I'm sure.

Waiting.

The unknown. The hopelessness. Empty. Useless.

Waiting.

I made drinks, offered food, tidied up, checked on the boys, made sure the phone was working, stared down the road and back again, checking for lights.

Midnight passed.

For hours we stared into a dark corner, each in our own mind, our own world. I watched Hana's skin grow paler and the bags under her eyes deepen. Seconds passed like minutes, like hours, like days. We jumped at every noise, hoped with every sound that he had returned. The room filled with silent prayers from muted lips.

We waited.

Some hours later we heard a car coming up the road. Just one car. It seemed we had all stopped breathing. Our bodies sat up slightly taller, our eyes leaped to each other, to the window, to the door. I looked at the worry on Hana's face, and I saw it mirrored in Fatima's. I hadn't thought, simply hadn't thought; her husband and child were out there too.

As we heard two doors slam, we stood up, our eyes

fixed on the door. And I saw and I heard the relief from Fatima as her family stepped back into the house, yet I saw the pity and the worry on her face as she turned to comfort Hana. She cared. I could see it flowing from her as she wrapped her arms around my auntie.

Saad spoke gently to Hana. They'd driven all over Baghdad, searching for Aziz's taxi, he said. They'd tracked down one of his customers, but he'd dropped them off safely in the city and gone on his way. They'd visited police stations, army checkpoints, banged on doors of street vendors and café owners, armed with a photo of Aziz and a description of his car. They'd asked at roadblocks, at restaurants, at bars and coffee houses.

No one had seen him.

They didn't know what else to do, they said, and for a while had just driven. Down roads lined with shops or houses, staring down alleyways and over bridges. But it was pointless, they said. So many streetlights were off again, the electricity down again, the city was in near darkness. A few of the houses with generators still leaked out light, but most had gone to bed and turned them off. There was no way to see. They would go out again in the morning, they replied.

With an embrace, and with hope for the next day,

they left, and as Hana closed the door behind them, her tears came. And I held her as she sobbed. And I rocked her, and I stroked her hair, and I offered her a tissue. But I said nothing. There were no words to give that would mean anything but hollowness.

Grief had pushed us together. First mine, then hers. And we sat together all night, dozing in and out of sleep, waiting, hoping, praying for the phone to ring or a knock at the door. Yet dreading what it might bring.

As I sat there in absolute darkness, I thought of my day. What my soldier had said, the hope he had given me, the possibilities it offered. And I listened to Hana's breathing next to me, for she was my family.

CHAPTER TWENTY-SIX

Morning came slowly, the sun creeping across the sky and bleeding through the windows, the warmth prickling my skin awake. Still in yesterday's clothes I headed for the door, staring out, down the street, at other houses, the mosque in the distance, a man dashing to work, the sound of cars on the next street, the city waking, lives continuing like yesterday, as if nothing had happened.

They didn't know Aziz. To them he was just another victim in a city full of victims.

I watched the long shadows reaching out, resting on everything. I wanted everything to stop, I wanted the city to stay like that, stilted, waiting, as we were.

I didn't want the sun to rise any higher. I didn't want the day to begin. I wanted to pause time right there. I didn't want the boys or Hana to wake. I didn't want to find out what had happened to Aziz; I didn't want to know, for I doubted the truth would bring any happiness. I wanted to stay in ignorance. I wanted my hopes for the future to stay as high as they were.

Yet I felt reality creeping towards me. I sensed the sun lifting, the shadows withdrawing. I felt misery and despair chasing us down. And there was nowhere left to hide.

I heard Hana's feet shuffle through, and I heard water pour into the kettle. I felt the day stretching ahead of me, and felt sick at the prospect of what it might bring.

I stood there still half an hour later, watching the city, listening to the sounds, breathing in the smells. I heard the boys wake, yet stayed where I was. A few minutes later I watched Saad and Fatima leave their house and walk over to me.

✤

There were no smiles on their faces, and I could feel the despair as we walked inside the house. It hovered in the air and over heads like a cloud. Saad watched the boys retreat to their rooms, and as he began speaking, Fatima rested her hand gently on Hana's.

He spoke in a clear voice, yet a low whisper, his tone

gentle, although his words were harsh.

He spoke of the Americans, *invaders* he called them, of when they first arrived in our city nearly two years ago, when their tanks and humvees streamed unforgiving towards our homes.

"About a year ago I went to visit my brother," he said. "He lives across the other side of the city. Lived, I should say. He's gone now. When I got there he was walking into his house carrying a spade. His hands were muddy, dirt on his face and sweat was pouring from him.

"I could see he looked upset; I asked him what the matter was. He explained to me, told me what had been happening near his house. As the Americans had stormed into Baghdad, their tanks and apaches had fired at any vehicle in their path. Indiscriminate. There seemed no reasoning. Then they left them, burning at the side of main roads, highways, residential areas, in front of houses, shops. These people, these civilians and families, trying to escape and find safety, were just shot at. Killed. Troops didn't even pause to consider if the vehicle was a threat. They were simply in the wrong place at the wrong time. Shoot first, no need to ask questions later."

I watched Hana's lip tremble as she listened.

"My brother told me that he spoke to the soldiers,

asking them to do something with the bodies. Take them to the morgue, or to the hospital, somewhere their families could find them at least. He said his neighbours asked too, but it was always the same response from the soldiers – not our problem. He told me he would stand outside his house, staring at the bodies inside the burnt-out cars, knowing he could not possibly leave them there. After a few days, he said, he realised he wasn't the only one. People were bothered about it, it upset them, upset their children, so the neighbourhood decided to do something. They dug graves for these innocents. They gave them a resting place. In their minds they gave them their last dignity. They dug together in the hard sun, whatever their background. In the hope that one day the families of these victims might come by – searching for brother, sister, cousin, wife, mother – they marked the graves.

"I stared at him, whether in disbelief or shock. How could this happen in *any* country? I had to see it for myself. I had to have it in my memory. Know it was true. Somehow record the tragedy of it in my head.

"He took me outside and we walked down the road, passing the remnants of the cars, some empty burnt-out shells, others pocked with bullet holes, smashed windscreens, doors hanging open. I peered closer at the blood-stained seats, some with belongings still inside, a child's doll, that day's newspaper. He led me round the corner, to what had been an empty space, where the children used to play, but now with piles of soil and dust in rows. The sight took my breath away. I moved towards one of the graves, a palm leaf wilting over it."

Hana's face was streaming with tears, her body gently rocking back and forth. I glanced to Saad, the point of his story somehow lost in his grief. I wanted to step in, tell him to stop talking, demand to know why he was telling my auntie this. I wanted to stop her pain, the woman I had never liked, who had taken my dreams away from me when I moved here. I wanted to help her, I wanted to protect her. But I was as caught up in this story and this man's grief as he was, and as Hana was.

I didn't want to know what was coming next, yet with some perverse curiosity, I needed to know. Not to wallow in his grief, or take pleasure from this suffering, but because of a hunger or a thirst for knowledge of what was happening to my country. As he had said himself – have it in my memory, record the tragedy of it in my head. These stories were part of tomorrow's history, and I wanted it remembered, truthfully, accurately, honestly.

And I wanted to know what this had to do with Aziz. But at the same time, I was disgusted, wanted to close my ears and stop these stories from taking root in my brain only to sprout out when I was by myself, when I was trying to sleep.

I wanted to know, I wanted to listen, but I wanted to protect myself too. I could no longer cope with all the stories of sadness and destruction. My head was pounding with everything that was going on. What about leaving? I had two days now. How could I leave with this happening? What about Aziz? What about Hana?

"On top of the grave, kept down by a stone, was a piece of cardboard. I lifted it, ADULT MALE, SMALL BOY, RED TOYOTA, it read. I moved across to the next grave, another palm leaf, another piece of cardboard; ADULT MALE, ADULT FEMALE, BLACK KIA. I moved to another, a licence plate stuck out of the ground, misshapen and charred, a piece of cardboard leaned next to it; ADULT MALE, ADULT FEMALE, TWO SMALL CHILDREN, WHITE VOLKSWAGEN.

"I stood, staggering backwards, my hand over my mouth, tears filling my eyes, my breathing shallow. I looked over the field, more than a dozen graves, marked with palm leaves, licence plates, labelled so their families could find them. My head swam with the incredulity of it.

"A woman in a burqa stumbled into the field, her grief was palpable, she rocked as she walked from grave to grave, muttering and praying. She stopped at one and fell to her knees, stretching her arms across the pile of dust, crying a name I couldn't make out, over and over again.

"I turned my back and walked away. I couldn't intrude on this woman as she mourned."

Hana wiped her face and lifted her chin a little. "Why are you telling me this?"

"We were told last night that this still happens now," he replied. "Car bombs, roadside bombs, IEDs, shootings, suicide bombs. So many are left to rot where they die, and still, if no one takes the bodies, the residents bury them." His voice was very quiet.

Hana stood up. "You will drive me there," she announced. "And if we don't find him, you will drive me around until we do. If there is one place where graves are made like this, then perhaps there are others. We will drive until we find my husband."

Saad frowned at her, bits of words and sentences

tumbled incoherently from his mouth about the dangers, but Hana, my Auntie Hana, flicked him away as if he was a fly struggling through heat.

"You do not come into my home, with my children and my niece, and tell me your horror stories then refuse to do anything about it. What did you expect me to do after telling me of such things? I will do as any loyal wife, and mother, and aunt would do. I will find my husband, the father of my children, dead or alive, and I will deal with what happens. If I am killed on the way, then it is God's will and I will be reunited with my family. Lina will come with us, my children can stay with your wife."

Saad had little option but to agree. Neither did I. God's will or not, I didn't want to go, I didn't want to die at the hands of some trigger-happy, gun-toting foreign soldier, or some bomb-wielding, religion-quoting fundamentalist, or some angry insurgent. I wanted to stick my hand up and say, *"Er, excuse me, Auntie Hana, if I didn't believe in God, and I die, it can't be His will, so it would be murder, and I'm sure you don't want me to be murdered, so I'll just stay here, and look after the house, if that's all the same by you."*

I didn't think that would go down too well.

God's will or no God's will, I did want to find Aziz.

So we went. Hana, myself, Saad and Jamail, piled into the car. *Two adult males, adult female, teenage female, white Volkswagen*, I thought to myself. Should I write it out now to save a job for the gravedigger later?

Travelling around the city was difficult. It took a long time to get not very far, our journey zig-zagging around roadblocks. The car, and ourselves, searched at every checkpoint. If the soldiers seemed all right and not too abrupt then we took the opportunity to ask them about Aziz and show his photo. There was lots of head shaking and I wondered if we all looked the same to them. As each one approached the car, I looked on with hope, daring to believe that it could be Steve, checking name tapes for those letters, looking for those blue eyes hiding behind dark glasses. I wished it was him who approached the car; that we would wind down the window, that he would lean down and see me, lift his glasses up, recognise me, smile at me. Offer his help to me.

But then, what if he did? *Hana would be pleased,* I thought, *but not pleased he wasn't marrying me and taking me away.*

After two hours we arrived at Saad's brother's neighbourhood.

I was told to stay in the car, but in my mind, that was

just as dangerous as walking around, and if we did find signs of Aziz in that makeshift graveyard, then I wanted to be there. I wanted to see the sign for myself and I wanted to be there for Hana. I needed to be there for Hana. So I went with them. I insisted.

I struggled out of the car with a heart that felt as if it was on fire. And I walked together to the dusty field hand in hand with Hana, stepping down row after row of dirt piles, cardboard notices, palm leaves and licence plates. My heart sank further with every grave we passed, my grief for strangers, unseen and unheard of. My grief for lives taken so young, so unexpectedly and so unfairly. My grief for a situation with no end in sight.

Young male, two males, one female, couple with two children, one child, male with young boy, one male, one female, one child. What about their families, missing them, searching for them? Wives missing husbands. Mothers missing children. Children missing siblings, missing parents.

A snapshot of the violence, the suffering and the pain. Stupid deaths; pointless. Civilian deaths? An inadequate phrase. These weren't merely civilians, these were people; fathers, mothers, sons, daughters, husbands, wives, friends, neighbours, colleagues.

They were someone.

Maybe the man who sells you bread in the mornings. The woman on the corner you see sweeping her house. The boy who kicked a ball into your garden. Your teacher from school. The beautiful receptionist you dream of looking like. The taxi driver you tipped. The man who held the door open for you.

People. Individuals.

I looked to Hana, the grief for these people lying at our feet, tearing at her, silent tears flooding her cheeks. And our eyes met, but neither of us had any words. What could anyone say?

I didn't think anything else in this war could shock me. But this? This was the stuff of nightmares, nightmares you can't wake from. It felt unreal and I didn't want to believe what I could see. But there it was, in front of me.

There was no grave for Aziz. I felt relief and frustration. I didn't want to find him here. I wanted him to come home, alive and well. He had only been missing a day; I thought of Mama, missing for years.

To know is to give it reason; to understand if not to empathise, to accept and then to eventually let go. Not knowing keeps a candle burning inside, hoping with every day that comes, praying like you really *do* believe, scared to let go.

Without a word, we climbed back into the car.

We thought about retracing Aziz's steps yesterday; but it wouldn't be easy. He worked for himself, picking up fares as he drove around, there was no record of who he picked up and where he went.

We went to a coffee shop he liked to go to, a place he and Papa spent time in together. A few of the people Saad spoke to came over to the car to offer Hana and myself their support and to wish us luck.

"We will pray for you. He will return. Inshallah."

We drove around all day. We visited hospitals, police stations, bars. We asked street vendors, café owners, taxi drivers. We showed his photo to soldiers, journalists and foreign TV crews.

Nobody had seen him or his car.

We arrived home just before the curfew and, with or without God's will, we were still intact.

It was me who heard the phone ringing as we stepped through the door, but for a second I didn't move, scared of what it could be. I thought about ignoring it, rushing everyone back outside with some excuse. If we didn't answer the phone, then it couldn't happen, they wouldn't talk to us, and they wouldn't tell us what we didn't want to hear.

But I moved towards it, and I picked up the receiver and with my eyes closed, I listened.

A deep voice, a male voice, my mind tried to make a picture of him in the darkness behind my eyes. I felt Hana close by, I felt eyes upon me, watching for my reaction, waiting to hear news. I opened my eyes to see a piece of paper and pen had been put in front of me. I took the pen and wrote.

Ransom. Fifteen thousand dollars. Two days. No police. No troops. Left in a bag in a bin. Zawra Park. Eleven o'clock.

Listening to him, writing the words, seeing them there, real on the page, made me feel physically sick and as he, whoever he was, finished the call, I dropped the receiver and ran for the bathroom. With my head hanging over the toilet, I heard Hana scream.

Aziz had been abducted.

I was so angry, so shocked. *Why Aziz?* my head screamed. Why him? What had he done? Such a lovely man. So kind and caring. Why? He wasn't an educated man, I wanted to scream to Hana. And they had given no reason. Had they been watching me with Steve? Was that why?

We couldn't go to the police; because the kidnappers would kill him. We couldn't go to the Americans; they might skew his abduction into a terror plot and arrest him if we ever got him back. We had no choice.

We were alone.

We had to pay the ransom.

Fifteen thousand dollars.

Exactly the amount my father had left for me, in the box in the wall. The money I was going to use to get out of the country.

I stared at the piece of paper in disbelief at the words I had written.

Hana wept and wept. Where were they, a small family, Aziz a taxi driver, Hana a housewife, going to find that sort of money?

"We have no savings," Hana cried. "Nothing. It's all gone, trying to survive this war. A generator, fuel, food, everything's so expensive now." I didn't know who she was talking to, maybe trying to justify it to herself, or to the god she so vehemently believed in, or to our neighbours, that she had no way of saving her husband's life. "I don't work. Where can I get the money from?" Words fell from her mouth and we could do little to console her.

"I can give you some," Saad said. "But only five hundred. I don't have much, and I must keep some in case this happens to us. You know that, you understand, I'm sure."

But I had the money. I had the answer. The key to Aziz's survival. To Hana not losing her husband, and the boys not losing their father, and to me, of course, not losing my dear uncle. Still hidden, in a tin, behind the broken brick, at the top of the wall, at the bottom of the stairs, in the basement. Fifteen thousand dollars.

I could fix this.

So why didn't I say the words?

Why did I stand there, mute, watching Hana suffer?

What about leaving? That truck would be waiting for me in two days. My escape. My future.

The dilemma bounced around my head. I had been promised this thing, this lifeline, this hope. And now? Now it was being torn away from me. I would have to stay. I thought how selfish I was. Surely if I cared, really cared, really loved Aziz, I wouldn't even have paused? I would have given the money with no hesitation. Aziz's life was at stake and I was withholding what was needed for his survival.

But I wanted to leave so badly.

CHAPTER TWENTY-SEVEN

Whatever happened to Sacha? Part VI

And Sacha went mad.

She crouched on the ground, rocking back and forth, shouting and wailing about bombs and orchestras, water and jewellery. She paced the floor, scraping her fingers along the walls, crying, ranting, then collapsing, exhausted, for a few moments. And her head would pound, images of her life gone by flashing before her; the last time she kissed her husband goodbye, the last time she waved her daughter off to school, her last day at work, the last time she walked across the foyer, her last images of Baghdad as she stepped from that door.

And the bag over her head, and the prison cell, and the pain, the humiliation, the fear.

Through her thoughts and the images flashing black and white and red behind her eyes, she could hear Nahla shouting at the guards, the words echoing, but making no sense.

"I'm scared," Sacha heard her cry. "She's crazy. She's going to kill me. She's going to kill herself."

She felt the sting of daylight as the lid was pulled off, and she heard the taunts and laughter from the guards, smelled a brief waft of clean air.

Am I dying? was the only question to come to her mind. *Finally. Finally. Am I dying?* This was the last thought before she collapsed to the floor, lying on the ground, not moving, not responding, her eyes open and glazed, sweat dripping from her forehead, circles around her armpits, a flood between her legs.

She couldn't hear Nahla's cries; relentless, begging and pleading, shouting and screaming that she was dead.

And she didn't feel herself hoisted out of the hole, or feel her body thrown to the ground. She didn't feel the sunlight dancing on her skin, the fresh air swirling around her, over her clothes and through her hair. She didn't notice a guard lean towards her, watching her chest and her lips, baulking at her smell, his hand over his mouth, disgust on his face.

And she didn't hear him mutter that she was still breathing, to dump her back in the hole.

As she hovered in and out of consciousness she heard a different voice, a different guard. "I'm not picking her up again," he said. "She can stay there. Leave her to die there."

As the orange and green shapes behind her eyelids grew, and as she breathed in the first fresh air in such a long time, she realised she was out of the hole. But before even the idea had sunk in, she felt a boot in her face, felt her body lurch to one side, felt her head hit the baked ground, and tasted the blood in her mouth.

She waited to die.

She lifted her swollen eyelids, two dark shapes against white sunlight, walking away.

She heard the metal lid clang shut and, standing in front of her, blocking out the sun, was another pair of boots. She waited for the pain in her face, in her chest or stomach or arms or legs.

Wherever he chose to kick her.

She waited for her hair to be pulled or her arm to be grabbed. A rag doll at the mercy of everyone.

But nothing came and her eyes carefully tilted upwards, slowly up his legs, past the gun at his waist, over his chest and to his face.

"She isn't dead," he shouted.

A reply came over the yard, carried on the slow breeze. "Will be soon."

Sacha watched the guard in front of her crouch down. She looked into his eyes, so young, and saw something there. Something like kindness, or compassion.

She opened her mouth to speak, tried to form the words, but none came. Her throat was dry, the words too difficult, too final.

"What?" he asked, leaning in, his face close to hers.

"Kill me," she whispered. "Please."

She watched his eyes. Watched him look away. Watched him following the backs of his colleagues. Waited for his reply.

But he shook his head.

And again she tried to speak, her mouth opening and closing, no sound coming.

And again he glanced to his colleagues. Still walking. Their backs still to him.

And Sacha watched. Hope and resignation filling her. Willing this man to help, to show her kindness that she hadn't seen in so long. She watched as he took a flask of water from his belt, twisting off the top, and she felt the best water of her life, the coolest water, the purest, touch her lips, trickle into her mouth and down her throat, and for a second, just a second, she felt alive again.

"Please," she said, her voice low, difficult, rasping. "I want to die. I want to go."

Her green eyes saw compassion flick over the guard's face as he looked at the state of the woman in front of him, and she wished she could tell him everything, her story for him to keep safe, to carry with him and tell the world, tell her husband, tell her child.

And tell them that she loved them, would always love them.

But she just stared at him, into him.

And from somewhere she found the strength to lift an arm, to stretch a hand, to reach her fingers into a pocket and pull out the necklace with a green stone and filigreed gold.

And holding it outstretched in her palm, her eyes stared into him.

And there were no tears.

There was only hope.

CHAPTER TWENTY-EIGHT

I remember there was no electricity that night. I remember we had no fuel for the generator. I remember watching as everyone slowly disappeared into the darkness that was growing, hiding us, the house, the furniture, inside it. I lit some candles, and the light flickered and danced on our faces; no romance in it or magic.

We were lost in our own worlds. I felt more weary, more frustrated, more confused and more angry, than I'd felt since the beginning of this war.

Saad said he would help Hana get some money together. He would visit colleagues of Aziz's, and friends. Hana would sell her jewellery, what little of it she owned. What was I to do? Fetch the tin with the money in it? Would Papa want me to do that for his brother-in-law? Would Aziz want me to do that?

I didn't know. I didn't know what to do. Either way I would lose. If I gave Hana the money, I couldn't leave. If I kept the money, I would be allowing Aziz to die. Was I selfish? I felt it.

What good had this war done? I had felt such hope for my country and my people, all that time ago. We were promised so much; things which were unimaginable to us then. I'm glad Saddam has gone. The man who took my mama away. I desperately am. And I await his trial with glee.

But what do we have in his place?

The night went on. The silence in the room bore down heavy on us all. What were we waiting for? Hana paced the room, back and forth, wringing her hands raw, sobbing, shaking, and we watched her, not knowing what else to do. In the early hours her eldest son came through, his eyes heavy from lack of sleep, his body unbalanced with tiredness. He told me to give her Valium.

He was eight years old; his brother six. I called him over to sit with me, and as he sat on my knee, I wrapped my arms around his tiny body. He whispered, inaudible to Hana in her world and worries, he told me about when the bombing was at its worse, when you worried for your life with every second, the explosions rocking the ground at your feet, cupboard doors clattering, glasses rattling to the edge of the table, that during those times, his brother would not settle. He screamed and cried, shouted and trembled. The first night they had tried to calm him, the second night Valium calmed him. He told me it was kinder, for him, for everyone. And he told me how Hana had held him on her lap, cuddling him, watching his chest rise and fall, and his anxiety drifted away.

I looked at this boy on my knee, who annoyed me so much with his pestering and shouting, his arguing and his moaning, and I thought the words could not have come from him. He stepped down, took my hand and led me to the bathroom.

"Give her two," he whispered, taking the box from the cupboard. I smiled at him and watched him go back to bed. Shortly after, Hana was sitting again in the living room, her tired, heavy eyes struggling against consciousness.

Saad and Fatima went home, with instructions to call if anything happened, if Hana or I needed anything, and the house fell into silence. I listened to it, my ears searching through it for sounds of life, for movement. I felt alone. But I knew I had to be strong.

I went up on to the roof and stared across the city. We slept on the roof sometimes, me and Papa, back at home, when the temperature was so high you couldn't bear to be inside at night. But when the war came and occupation began, it was noisy at night, it was dangerous, and being out there, surrounded by the noise, watching the explosions light up orange behind your closed eyelids, was too much to bear. I missed those heady nights from before.

But as New Year's Day left us, the air was chill and I pulled a blanket around myself, looking out across my city. We had seen no fireworks that New Year. We had heard only explosions. And we had seen no singing or dancing. It had escaped our house.

Staring across the city, there was little to see other than darkness. So many people without power, and so little fuel for generators. Everything was turned off. I wondered if the Green Zone had power, the army bases. Probably, I decided. I wished my eyes could search through the darkness and find where Aziz was. He was somewhere out there, I was sure. I wished I could close my eyes and think really hard, and lift my arms up and my fingers would stretch out, my index finger would point, and I would open my eyes, and that would be where he was.

I could name the street, find the building and the room. I wished.

I didn't know what to do. I didn't know where to find help, who to ask, what to say.

A few car headlights were visible in the distance, and I watched them as they turned left or right, continued straight a while, the streets and corners and junctions barely distinguishable in the darkness. I wondered who they were, where they were heading and I wished they were heading here, and that inside was Steve.

I wanted to talk to him, to tell him what was happening to my family, to ask for his help. Not because he was a soldier and not because he was an American, an occupier, an invader. But because, regardless of all that, to me he felt like a friend, and at that moment, it felt like I needed a friend.

But the headlights didn't head towards me, and they probably didn't have Steve inside. But a friend, I thought; and I thought, I must see Layla before I leave, because in the morning there would be only one day left before I had to make my decision, between my uncle's life, and my own.

CHAPTER TWENTY-NINE

I slept fitfully. I remember waking, feeling too hot, waking again, feeling too cold. I remember hearing footsteps and tears, mumblings of others dreaming, heavy sighs upon them waking.

But for me there were no dreams. Not of Aziz, not of money, and not of trucks or boats or new countries. No decisions arriving subconsciously into my brain, delivered by a messenger who knew better what to do than I did.

I had a day. One day to get the money. One day to give it.

One day before I left.

Or one day to save Aziz.

By the time the sun had set on that day, I could be gone. And Aziz could be dead. Or I could be at home.

And Aziz could be alive. There was no choice when it was said like that. No decision to be made. How could I even contemplate leaving?

But would they really kill him? I wondered how much money Hana had already. And she had the rest of the day to find more. And Saad and Fatima would help. Surely? Wouldn't that be enough?

My mind swam back and forth with indecision. I wished I could talk to someone. Talk it over with someone. With Layla? But no, I couldn't burden her with all that. After not seeing her for so long, to turn up on her doorstep with that? I couldn't do it.

I waited a few hours, until Hana was up and friends were with her. I told the oldest child I wouldn't be long, told him not to mention that I'd gone, and I slipped out of the house.

I had thought about where I must go, what I must do and what I must say, but now, I felt at a loss. I was scared. It wasn't safe, and the chance that I wouldn't return home again was very real. Could I really do this?

I headed for the gas station, thinking that maybe, just maybe, he'd be there again. I remembered that day, that meeting. Not the first. But the first that I could remember with fondness; my hands shaking as I passed him some chai, those bright blue eyes searching into mine. Those first moments, those first words, a sparkle of something I hadn't felt in so long, of friendship, of hope. And as I bungled along with my abaya over my body and my hijab over my head, without much of a plan other than of finding him, I thought of everything that had happened since that meeting.

I kept my head down as I turned the corner, excitement daring to lift in my chest. And I waited as long as I could before looking up, keeping that feeling alive, but when I did, when my eyes scoured through the dust, and the cars, and the people, there were no troops, there was no Steve.

Where should I go? What should I do? Where would I find him? My head swam with thoughts and questions, and I wandered, down streets, across roads, past shops, over bridges, stupidly and thoughtlessly, my desperation rising and my fear eating me that I would not make it home. What was I thinking? Walking around alone, through streets and across areas I knew were dangerous? But in my mind there was only one reason and only one answer; I had to find him.

My feet ached; sweat dripped from me. I was scared. I didn't know where I was, or where I was heading. I looked up and found myself in front of the Assassin's Gate, the entrance to the Green Zone; home to soldiers and diplomats, bureaucrats and journalists. A safe haven for them, guarded by soldiers. I walked towards it, the sunlight reflecting from its sandstone, trees lining its approach, soldiers guarding the safety that lay within. I could see barbed wire and tanks, blockades and guns.

Was he in there, somewhere in the expanse which lay beyond those guards? Wondering about me and my trip to the west? I tried to talk to a soldier, a guard. What was his full name? they asked. I don't know, I replied, he's Sergeant Stevens, everyone calls him Steve. What battalion is he with? What business do you have with him? What's his rank and number?

I don't know, I don't know, I don't know, came every reply I gave.

They mocked me, laughed at me, pointed their guns at me and told me to leave. But I stood my ground and refused. What had got into me? I didn't know. I have to speak to him, I told them. They shook their heads at me, warning me. But what choice did I have?

I stared at one of them as he marched towards me, his eyebrows lowered, his lip sneered, disgust dripping from him, his gun raised.

He looked like he was going to hurt me and suddenly I was struck by fear. A brighter fear than ever before. I sucked in breath, hot and panicky.

And the pain hit me. And I fell to the floor.

My eyes were closed, my vision flashing white.

I lifted my hand to my cheek and felt warm blood running down, staring at it on my fingers.

The soldier stood above me, the butt of his gun raised above my head. I put my arms up to protect myself, and my head spun as I struggled to my feet. But the soldier didn't back up, he stood over me, forcing his way towards me, forcing me back with his sheer presence. I shied backwards, stepping away, his face leering into mine, his spit showering me, his dark glasses obscuring his face, reflecting back my fear. I stumbled again, on to the floor, my hands, my face, my clothes covered in dirt, blood dripping down my cheek.

He grabbed hold of my arm, his fingers digging into my skin through my clothes, and he dragged me away; my feet not fast enough to pull myself upright, my legs bare, scrambling. He threw me on to the floor and strode away, and for a moment I stayed there, watching him go, my skin sore and grazed, gravel stuck into my shins, my face bruised and bleeding, embarrassment pouring from me as people walked around me, avoiding me.

I wanted to sit there, stay there. For the ground to open up and swallow me whole. I felt vulnerable. Felt shame dripping from me. But I stood up, wiped my face and brushed myself down. And I took a deep breath and turned away from the Green Zone, and I was determined to carry on.

I was shaking as I headed back across the river, the weight of a thousand worlds on my shoulders, the responsibility of one man's life in my hands. My face was sore, my hands covered in dried blood, my body ached, but I walked on with my head high, staring into the face of every soldier I saw, at every tank, every humvee, hoping to see him.

I had no idea how long I'd been gone, but my stomach growled and my throat burned. I knew I was running out of time and options. The day was disappearing, dwindling away as was my life there.

I was nearing home when I saw them. What possessed me to approach them, I really don't know. Maybe that I could be humiliated no more. Or that they would do no worse than the guard had. Or perhaps it was desperation. Hopelessness.

I didn't know what they were doing – their truck

had stopped, the engine still turning over, a soldier still at the wheel. A few were walking about, one smoking, glancing down the street, a couple talking to an Iraqi, another few standing around, chatting.

As I walked over, one nodded to the other, pointing in my direction. He took off his glasses as I approached, squinting at me through the sunlight.

"I'm looking for Sergeant Stevens," I said. I felt his eyes rest on the gash on my cheek. "Everyone calls him Steve. He's from Massachusetts."

"Why?" he asked.

"Hey," a second yelled, lifting his hand to me. "You got any chai today?"

"I need to speak to him," I replied to the first.

"'Bout that?" he asked, nodding to my face.

I shook my head. "My uncle's been abducted."

The second one strolled over. "Y'all look the same to me, but you, with your pretty face, I remember you." He stopped, staring at my cheek, frowning.

"Her uncle's been abducted," the first said with a sigh. It wasn't big news; they had heard it all before.

I looked at them, taking in their faces, their mannerisms, their voices. I didn't know the first. The second I remembered. I read his name tape, Manning.

"I'm looking for Steve," I repeated. "I need to speak to him."

Manning took a step towards me.

"I don't know his full name. I don't know what battalion he's with. I think he's a sergeant. Sergeant Stevens. Everyone calls him Sergeant Steve. He's from Massachusetts. He's got a sister, she goes to university…"

He nodded, his hand raised to pause me. "You mean Jerry," he said. "Jerry Stevens. Hated his first name. Liked Steve. Bit taller than me. Blue eyes, bit of a quiet voice, blond?"

I nodded.

"And you used to come to the gas station, with chai? Chat to him and that?" I nodded again.

He took a deep breath and leaned towards me. "Wasn't he helping you with something else?" he whispered.

I nodded. "But I can't do it, I don't think I can. The money… I have the money, but there's the ransom… for my uncle… I can't… can't do both… I don't know…" I stopped, blinking back the tears, swallowing the lump in my throat.

I wanted to see Steve, a friendly face, I wanted him to hold me and tell me everything would be all right, even though I knew it wouldn't. I wanted to talk to someone, to cry to someone while they listened, and while they cared. And I had no one.

Manning shook his head, looked back at me and sighed. "He's gone," he said. "Yesterday. It was real sudden."

I didn't move. I focused on his mouth, watching the words coming out, the world spinning around us.

"What?" I breathed.

Manning shrugged. "He got a call from back home, couple of days ago. His dad was sick, real sick. There was a chopper available so they sent him home. Lucky bastard."

Tears spilled down my face, but I didn't know why I was crying. Relief that he wasn't dead? Frustration that he had left? Loneliness?

"Hell, he was gonna tell you. I thought he had. Thought he'd been to see you." He shrugged again. "Maybe didn't get the chance," he said.

We stood together while the engine rumbled, and the other soldiers chatted and the Iraqi man waved his arms around trying to be understood. But my ears heard nothing but the silence between Manning and myself. I thought back to the last time I saw Steve. Did he know then that he was going? Why didn't he say anything?

Why didn't he tell me?

"I can't do anything about your uncle," he said. "You should go to the police."

"They said they'd kill him if we did that."

"Then pay the ransom."

"Then I can't leave."

He shrugged. "Nothing's ever black and white," he said.

"No," I whispered.

"You meant a lot to him, to Steve. He liked you. Hell, I'm sure he still does. But, y'know, even if he was here, I don't know if he could do anything to help."

I glanced up to him, watching him fold a stick of chewing gum into his mouth. I gave the tiniest of nods, turned and walked away. Back to the house, to Hana, to the boys, and to the decision I had to make.

❖

I saw Hana at the window as I approached, saw her eyes rest on mine, the worry on her face lift for just a second and I realised what I had done. For a moment I stopped walking and we stared at each other. Then I stepped into the house, knowing what was to come, and her temper hit me.

"Where have you been?" she shouted, her face close to mine, anger pouring from her, her eyes flicking over my face, my cheek, down to my clothes, to my hands. "What have you been doing?"

I didn't know how to answer. How could I tell her the truth? How could I lie? I stood there, my mouth open, no words to say.

"Don't you think there's enough on my mind without having to worry about you? Don't you care what I'm going through? What's happening to this family? To me? To the boys? Don't you care what's happening to Aziz?"

"I… I'm sorry," I muttered.

"Sorry? You've been gone all day, we had no idea where you were, what had happened to you. No way of finding you and that's the only thing you can say? I should hope you are sorry. I was worried sick, Lina."

"You don't need to worry about me," I replied, my voice small, insignificant.

She stared at me, a strange look mixed with disbelief, anger, hatred and relief. "How could I not worry about you? Anything could've happened. And something did, by the look of your face. How did I know you hadn't been abducted as well? Killed in an attack?"

"I didn't want to tell you I was going out in case you tried to stop me."

"And I would have. It's not safe, Lina, and you know that. What would your papa think of me? What would he think of you?"

We stood in silence. Did I have anything to say other than the apology I had tried? She was right, of course. It was dangerous. And I knew that. It was a stupid thing I did, but I would do it again.

I lifted my eyes to see her staring at me. "What happened to your face?" she asked, her voice lower, quieter, calmer.

I took a deep breath. "I was looking for someone," I replied. "Someone I thought might be able to help us. But I couldn't find him." I touched my cheek. "It was a soldier," I whispered.

And I'm sure I saw her expression change. Sure it softened slightly, relaxed maybe, sure her shoulders lowered, and her face lightened. I waited for her to move towards me, hoped she would take me in her arms and hold me tight, tell me she wouldn't let anyone hurt me again.

But she didn't.

Instead she closed her eyes and sighed; turned away

with her head low. "Clean yourself up," she muttered. "And don't do it again."

She left the room and I didn't know what to think or what to do, because I knew I had to do it again, I knew that tomorrow I had to get the money. Whatever my decision was to be.

CHAPTER THIRTY

I woke early the next morning, when the sun had barely risen, and I pulled the covers over my head, wanting to stay there, for sleep to take me again, hide me from my indecision and my guilt. My failing hope and my lost excitement.

My interrupted life.

I knew what I should do. But I knew what I wanted to do. I had so little time left before that decision had to be made.

I dragged the covers off the bed, keeping them wrapped around me, and sat at the window, peering out for maybe the last time. I flicked over the pages of my sketchbook, stopping at the last one, at Steve. I sighed. I missed him, and I really wanted to, really *needed* to, speak to him. But I was alone, and this decision was for me.

I lifted my pencil and on a clear page tried to sketch the view. But what was there to see? A burnt-out car, a shell, the body blackened. Glass strewn around it sparkling in the light. Tyres melted around the rim, the road around it charred.

Shop doorways boarded up, metal bars at windows twisted out of shape. Black graffiti sprayed on concrete walls. Paths and pavements broken and crumbling into roads. Cardboard boxes and broken bin liners spilling out rubbish.

My pages filled with heartache.

I closed my eyes, and in my imagination I strolled through Zawra Park, dipping my fingers into the water of the fountains, the grass tickling my bare feet, the sun dancing on my face as I watched the theatre in the open air.

I strolled home down busy streets with smiling people. Jostled through markets with their bright colours of bananas, oranges, lemons; their piles of cinnamon, cumin, paprika.

I wished I could stay there. In my imagination.

But guilt dragged me back. I could hear footsteps pacing, cups and pots clanging, erratic voices. I dressed quickly and headed downstairs. Peering around a corner,

I saw Fatima in the kitchen, saw her turn the kitchen taps and heard the pipes groan; another day without water. Hana stared, vacant, her red eyes fixed on nothing.

I went back to my room, took my bag from under my bed and, again, slipped out of the house. I had thought about leaving a note this time, but couldn't think what to write. I had thought about asking Hana's permission, but knew it would be refused, and I had to go, simply had to go. There was no option. I had to get to the house. I had to get to the money. I looked at my watch, the hours, the minutes ticking by, counting down to my decision.

I hurried through the streets, my body cloaked to the floor, a niqab covering my face this time. I hated myself for wearing it; I felt a fraud, a traitor to my own religion. And I was clumsy. The long material of my skirt caught on my feet. I stumbled on kerb edges, tripped on loose stones. I didn't glide as some girls seemed to; I was neither sophisticated nor graceful nor elegant. I was a rain cloud, an ink blot, a dark stain. But this wasn't about religion; this was about survival. I was hidden, I was anonymous and I was protected. At least somewhat.

And when I arrived, I was still alive.

I watched my house, my home, approaching from a distance. A speck, growing, its windows and doors smiling at me, welcoming me back. And as I stepped through the door, I felt the memories envelop me, everything as it was, paused in time, as if waiting for our return. And here I was. Just me.

I wandered through the house and in my mind I could see Papa, sitting in his favourite chair, a book across his lap, his eyes nodding closed. I could see him stroll through the back door with a spade in his hands and a smile on his face, Aziz in the garden behind him. I could see him standing at Mama's wardrobe, his fingers holding the fabric to his face, his eyes closed as he inhaled.

And I could see Layla walk into the house with her school bag on her shoulder, glancing up to the clock as I slipped on my shoes, and as I peered through the windows covered still in tape and dust, I could see her brothers playing, a football kicked down the street, a shout to their friends.

And I could see Mama laying in bed, a baby in her arms, her face a wide, bright smile, and I could see Papa sitting next to her, smiling down at the baby, at me. And I batted back my tears, as I saw Papa lean in to kiss Mama, to kiss their baby, to kiss me.

I closed my eyes as the memories of my life, of my family, and of the stories I'd been told, seeped through me. I revelled in them. I travelled back in time and age as I watched them and when I opened my eyes again, they were still there, but hiding just below the surface, in every room.

I didn't feel Papa with me as I headed into the basement, rays of light from the small window stretching through the gloom and dust. And as I dragged a chair over to the stairs and pulled the tin out from behind the broken brick, I heard nothing but the heavy thudding of my heart, and felt nothing but my own fear.

I flinched against the sunlight as I emerged from the house with the tin in my bag, locking the door behind me, locking away my memories, and I paused for a moment, looking over to Layla's house. Should I visit her? I so desperately wanted to. I wanted to share everything with her that was going on in my life. Tell her about Steve, about leaving, about Aziz, about the money. But where would I start? What would she think of me when I told her? I didn't know what I thought of myself any more. I missed her, our friendship, our lives together.

With a sigh I walked on, a black mark stuttering through the sunlit day. I was horribly conscious of the money in my bag, how much there was, how if anyone knew it was there, they would steal it from me for sure.

My decision loomed ahead of me; I was torn. I pulled the piece of paper from my pocket, the instructions Steve had given me, the time, the place. I headed further into the city. I crossed the river. I saw Haifa Street looming. A dangerous place. I didn't want to be near it. I moved into a side street, not far from my pick-up point now, and the truck that was to take me to my new future, my safety and my hope.

My breathing was shallow, fear and nervousness and anxiety squeezing my chest. I could feel sweat on my hands and I wiped them down my clothes. I felt the heaviness of the tin in my bag, thought of all that money inside it. I kept walking. The Grand Mosque loomed ever closer, cranes above it, still unfinished, and I knew I would soon be at the pick-up point. I glanced at my watch, ten minutes left.

And the mosque became nearer and nearer, and I could see a truck pulled up at the roadside, exhaust fumes belching out. Someone approached it, a bag on their back, an envelope in their hands, passed to the man standing to the side.

I felt my pace slow. I stared at the man stood waiting, stared at his face, his receding hair, his long nose, his stained teeth. And I couldn't breathe. The money burned in my bag. I saw Aziz in my head. Papa. Mama. Layla. Hana. The boys. I saw my house, my home, my city, my school, my friends. I saw my memories. I felt the warmth of them. Home. Friendship. Family. Love.

My feet stopped. And I looked.

My breathing stopped. And I stared.

I felt the paper still in my hand.

My contact for Steve, my escape from here.

I crumpled it up and dropped it to the floor.

And with the heaviest of sighs, of fear, of relief, of disappointment, of resignation, I walked on.

CHAPTER THIRTY-ONE

Whatever happened to Sacha? Part VII

He held the necklace in his palm: green stone, filigreed gold. He remembered the day, *that* day. Pats on the back from his colleagues, low whistles at his booty. He had gone up in their esteem. And as the youngest and newest guard there, always made fun of, always given the worst jobs, how pleased he was at the time.

But how many years ago now? And still her face loomed in his dreams, her eyes pouring into his. Her begging. Her pleading. The scene still played over in his head, over and over and over, but now the pain he felt, felt so much worse.

It woke him in the mornings. Followed him all day.

It laid with him in the evenings. Kept sleep from him.

Ate him. Lived off him.

And still the memories of that place haunted him. The actions he took under orders, how wrong he knew they were, even then. But still he did them. With his conscience turned off, hoping to keep his guilt at bay. What else could he have done? What were his options? He knew then, and knew all the years following as guilt chased him, hid in the darkness waiting for him, bearing down on him, laughing at him, that he had had no choice. He could not have refused.

The memory of her, of that day, of the promise he had made, never left him. All his guilt from all his actions in that place, focused on her and that promise.

He rubbed his finger against the green stone, wrapped the chain around his hand, the guiltiest piece of jewellery he'd ever touched.

He should've sold it then.

Instead he'd kept it like a medal of honour.

But what honour was there?

He'd thought about giving it to the girlfriend he'd had at the time, but something had stopped him. The same thing that had stopped him selling it, and kept it hidden in a drawer away from sight; his or anyone else's. And now, now that Saddam's police and the army were disbanded, now he had no job, no income, no future, now he felt he could really do with the money, and no one would be interested in it, or buy it, even if he found the will to sell it.

There was no need or desire or money for expensive jewellery. Bread, water, fuel and a generator were far more valuable.

Time stagnated around him, and memories returned like ghosts. Greying mist turning from invisibility into something tangible, clawing at his soul.

The woman's face returned to him frequently, and not just in dreams or nightmares, her eyes pleaded with him, seeing right into him, past the training and the regime and stared right at *him*. He knew what he should do, what he had been putting off for five years, but his courage evaded him. Used up, he thought, on that day, yet still unsure if he'd done the right thing.

But maybe, just maybe.

Maybe if he did return it, it would mean he could sleep again at night. Not see her face every morning, feel her walking with him every day, waiting. Not see her eyes staring into his every time he looked at that stone. With some kind of thanks, but with impatience, with anger.

And maybe, just maybe, it would help them, her husband and her child, to know what had happened to her. What he had done. But fear clawed at him. What would they say to him? What would they do? How would they feel? He was not sure if they would be angry or relieved, to finally know.

But surely they would know already? Someone would've told them?

He thought his argument around in circles, but he knew what he had to do. It was inevitable. He pulled open a drawer, lifting out that piece of paper, unfolding the creases of those years, staring down at his own handwriting.

The names, the address.

And he knew.

CHAPTER THIRTY-TWO

The niqab hid my tears as I walked home, my baggy clothes hid the sobs racking my body. But neither went any way to concealing the guilt that tore at me. And the pain. I cried for a million reasons, yet with every tear came guilt that I was crying at all.

There should've been no decision to make and there should've been no tears to shed. I should've been smiling that Aziz would be coming home. And I was glad, really I was.

But my last hope, given to me by two men so special to me, I was to give away. What would Papa think? What about Steve?

I ran through conversations in my head of what to tell Hana. I could've saved her from all that pain, all that heartache; trying to find the money, begging neighbours, friends, Aziz's colleagues. I could've spared her all that. And I had no reason, other than my own uncertainty, and my own selfishness.

I arrived back to a house silent with trepidation, expecting the anger Hana had shown me the day before. I walked through to find her at the kitchen table, a pile of grubby bank notes in front of her, her head in her hands. Fatima with her. Saad counting the money.

"I don't know what to say," he whispered. "There's nowhere near enough."

Hana didn't look up. Her grief, her worry, her fear, was palpable, the house was thick with it, it poured from her. I sat next to her and took her hand. She looked at me and I lifted off my niqab and smiled at her through my own disappointment and pain.

She frowned at me as I unzipped the bag on my lap and pulled out the tin. And her mouth fell open as I lifted off the lid and the money sprouted forward, crumpled, creased, dirty American bank notes, forced into a tin far too small.

"An educated man gave it to me," I said.

I felt all eyes upon me, on my bruised face and my red eyes, and I blushed, ashamed and embarrassed.

"But it was his love that taught me to do the right thing with it," I whispered.

I looked into Hana's eyes, at all of her loss and suffering, her love for her family, for me even, and I smiled and I really meant it.

✣

I went with Saad and Jamail to drop off the ransom money. In their car. Safety in numbers, we thought. I stared through the window at the streets I had only recently walked down. We avoided roadblocks, as was usual, but were stopped at checkpoints, keeping the money hidden under a seat.

We drove past the mosque, past the very spot the truck had been parked, gone now, on its way out of the country, as I could've been. And I thought of my decision. And I thought of Aziz; my big, cuddly uncle, with his piano-key teeth still stained with tobacco, and his smile that split his face in two and lifted my spirits soaring to the sky.

There really had been no decision to make.

We dropped the money off in Zawra Park, as ordered, left in a bin. I wondered if they were watching us, hidden in the bushes, sat on a bench, waiting near the grass.

Their eyes everywhere. I hoped they were. I hoped they were seconds behind us, taking that money, releasing Aziz, returning him home.

And then, we waited.

Hana paced and cooked and cleaned. I helped and played with the boys. We shot looks at the phone every few minutes. We glanced out of the windows, peered down the street, made excuses to go outside to look. We paused when a car went by, waiting, listening to it get louder, waiting, hoping it would stop, waiting, sighing as it didn't and returning to work.

We waited, and time went on and the sun went down.

The boys went to bed. Hana took some Valium and fell asleep in the chair. Darkness engulfed me again.

I don't remember falling asleep, I don't know what time it was, I just remember waking, stiff and uncomfortable. The silence felt wrong. I threw a blanket over Hana and tiptoed around the house. The air was thick and musty. I eased the door key around in the lock, and stepped out into the cold.

I stayed close to the house, a robe wrapped around me. The slightest breeze lifted through my hair and danced over my skin. I breathed it in. I could hear something. Faint, barely a whisper, my ears straining. A car engine. *Could it be?* I dared to think. I ran to the low wall surrounding the garden, peering over, I could see nothing. Yet I could hear it. I waited as it became louder, then, in the distance, I saw a pair of white headlights shining towards me. Surely not, I thought, not now, not in the middle of the night. I moved back towards the house, keeping low, hidden, listening, waiting.

And it kept getting louder. And I didn't know what to do. Whether to wake Hana, find a torch, to stand in the road waving, or to go inside, to lock the doors, to hide, and so, instead, I just crouched there, on the floor, next to the wall, with my heart thumping out of my chest.

The car slowed, the headlights brighter, and it pulled up, right next to the house, beams of light casting down the street, shadows across the garden. I heard the car door open. I held my breath, desperate for them not to hear me, not to find me. I saw the silhouette of a man, another door opened, and I heard something thud on the floor, something heavy. And the car door slammed shut. The engine revved. The headlights drew off. The car disappeared.

Silence covered me again. Dare I move? I didn't know what to do. What had been dumped out of the car? I was afraid I already knew the answer. With a heart as heavy as lead, I stood up. I went back into the kitchen, taking the oil lamp from the table, lighting it with a match from the drawer.

The light flickered, the shadows dancing on the walls and cupboards. I lowered the glass over the flame, held the lamp by the base and stepped outside. I edged slowly to the gate; my breathing heavy, my heartbeat a drum. The gate creaked open and I stared at my feet as they shuffled around the corner. I didn't want to look up. I didn't want to see what I thought I was going to find.

I lowered the lamp, stretching out my arm, tiptoeing forward, bending down to my knees. And there he was.

Oh, Aziz.

My beloved, cherished, wonderful, smiling, happy, Uncle Aziz. Lying on the ground. Thrown in a heap without a care. I held the lamp to his face, ran my fingers along his skin, covered in bruises and cuts, his eyes swollen shut, blood dried on his lips. I brushed his hair from his face, barely recognisable, but it was him. And he wasn't moving.

Panic rose in me. I rested the lamp on the floor and ran my hands over him. He can't have been killed, I shouted in my head. *He can't have, we paid the ransom, he can't be dead.* Tears poured down my cheeks and I rested my head on his chest, snuggled into the crook of his neck, wanting to feel his heartbeat, hear his booming voice, feel his arms wrap around me and hold me.

What had they done to him? Why? We paid the ransom, I wanted to shout, we paid it. I didn't understand. Why? I wanted to scream, why have you done this?

Then I felt his chest lift.

I caught my breath, sat up, my hands over my mouth. Daring to believe.

I watched his chest fall. Saw his lips move. His eyes flicker behind their swollen lids.

I touched his face. Put my ear to his mouth, felt the tiniest breath on my skin, heard the faintest whisper of my name. "Lina?" he breathed.

And I cried.

And I sobbed. Relief filling me.

When I heard Hana's feet running up behind me, and I turned to see the torment in her eyes, I could barely mouth the words, "he's alive," through disbelief, and shock and the emotion shaking at my body.

I watched her fall to her knees, take her husband's face in her hands and stare into him with love I had never before witnessed. I saw her tears of relief fall on to his broken skin.

She smiled. She kissed him. She held him.

And sometime later, when we had carried him into the house with help from our neighbours, when we had strapped his broken leg, bathed his cuts, stared into his eyes with concern that he may never regain his sight, when Hana had fed him, and the boys had cuddled him, we went back to bed with a strange sense that sometimes, sometimes, despite all this chaos, sometimes the right thing can happen.

CHAPTER THIRTY-THREE

The following days seeped into weeks and it turned into February again. Although every time I looked at Aziz I was reminded of how lucky we were to have him back, when I looked closer I realised, as we all did, that he was not the same man as the one who was taken. His eyesight had gone, his personality had changed. Nerves, worry and fear had replaced his sense of humour, his booming laugh and his wide smile.

I missed the man he had been. We all did.

Silence from him had become normality. He refused to speak of what had happened and we tiptoed around him, and each other, scared of saying or doing the wrong thing, all of us lost in our own worlds of frustration, hoping that time would ease him from his shell, dim the memories and help him become Aziz again.

I thought about the money, thought about how it could've changed things, where I could be, what I could be doing, and although I knew I had made the right decision, I was angry. Angry at everything and everyone. My thoughts spun in the same decreasing circles every day. Mama, Papa, Steve, Aziz too, I missed them all. My home, my family, my friends, and my education. My life. Everyone's life here. Broken and bleeding.

A promise of freedom and democracy, lost in war.

❖

The beginning of spring came. Two years since the war had begun, two months since our first election, my first vote, yet things were no better. Casualties and deaths increased. Lawlessness. I was scared. We all were. Again, fear was our constant. More American troops poured in and I would look at their faces in hope, their names across their chests, praying to see again the man who had offered me hope, the man whom I missed so much.

It was a Saturday afternoon when I found the photo. I was trying to fit yet more of the boys' drawings in the cupboard, when I noticed it wedged down the side. I pulled it out and felt a smile creep on to my face. There we were, all of us, captured. A birthday, maybe, or Christmas, a paper hat balanced on Papa's head, me laughing at him. Hana and Mama sitting together on the floor – one of the boys, a toddler, grabbed for the camera, the other, a baby in Hana's arms. Aziz stood at the back, his arms outstretched, his customary smile across his face.

I loved them all.

"Christmas 1998," Hana said from behind me. "The last Christmas with your Mama."

"I would've been twelve," I replied. "I don't remember it."

She peered at the photo from over my shoulder. "That's a shame." She paused and looked at me and I saw the sadness in her eyes. She pulled open the cupboard door and lifted out some photo albums. "Come on," she said.

And we sat together at the table, poring over photos of aunts and uncles, grandparents and cousins, photos of Hana and Mama's sisters and brother, photos of their friends from childhood, of their husbands as they met them. I could see how they'd changed, how my home had changed, how Baghdad had changed. And I wondered what was left to come for us all.

We paused on one of Mama. "That must've been before I was born," I said. "She's not wearing her necklace."

Hana nodded.

"Papa told me the story," I replied.

We fell into an awkward silence, then Hana turned to me. "Lina, it's going to be very difficult, finding the money to live and to eat. Aziz can't work. I have no savings any more."

"I know, Auntie Hana," I replied. "I'll do what I can, I'll work and bring some money in."

She nodded. "We'll need you to. But perhaps, when you're not working, if you've got the time, you might like to think about going back to your studies."

I froze, staring at her. Was this really the woman I had hated so much? Who forbade me to go to university? Who believed education would only bring trouble?

"I couldn't bear to lose you," she whispered, "but I know there is no sense here any more. I know you could be killed going out to get bread, coming home from work, here in this house, in your own bed." She took a deep breath. "Aziz tried to talk me into letting you go," she said. "And I think that's what they would've wanted, your Mama and Papa."

I threw my arms around her and cried. "Thank you," I said. "Thank you, thank you, thank you." I pulled away from her. "And Mama will thank you too when she comes home, I'm sure."

She rested her hand on mine and stared at me. "Lina, I really don't think…"

And I knew what she was going to say, but I didn't want to hear it, not at that moment. While I didn't know, while we didn't say it, I could still hope.

"I think I'd like to go down to the house," I said. "The old house, if that's all right. Pick up some things. Maybe get the photos from there before they're ruined."

Her frown meant no, but I didn't wait for her reply.

CHAPTER THIRTY-FOUR

Whatever happened to Sacha? The final part.

The necklace burned in his pocket as he drove into Baghdad and across the city, the piece of paper resting on the passenger seat, though he knew it by heart, knew which direction to go, which streets to take. Knew their names, Lina and Joe, the words that had echoed in his head for years.

Over and over he played out the conversation in his head. How he would tell them, the words he would choose, and he knew that he must tell them the truth, exactly how it happened. He owed them that much. He owed that much to himself.

He had seen pictures of Baghdad on the television, watched news reports, seen the explosions, the carnage, seen it to a lesser degree in his own nearby town, but still he felt the shock hit him as he drove down the battered streets, saw the dejection on people's faces, the houses falling down, piles of rubble that were homes, rubbish piled at corners. He wound down the window and the heat seared through his air-conditioned car.

He heard the growl of the generators, the roar of a tank coming up behind him, heard the quick shots of a machine gun some distance away, but he ducked his head and still his fingers clenched on to the steering wheel.

Nothing, no pictures, no videos, no news reports, no stories, could've prepared him.

He drove across the city, past troops and guards, sweat covering him as with each checkpoint he feared being searched, the necklace being found, taken off him for whatever reason they decided.

"What are you doing in Baghdad?" they might ask. "What is your business here?" But what could be his reply? A made-up story of visiting some friend, some relative? He knew no one in Baghdad. His mind pictured the necklace in his pocket, pictured handing it back, and he kept going, driving, hoping to reach the house.

He turned into the street, following the car in front

of him. His stomach flipped, nerves attacked him, his hands shook. He glanced across to the piece of paper, checking he had the right place, but he knew already that he had. His attention drifted from the road and he braked quickly as he looked up, too close to the car in front.

But his thoughts and worries stayed with the necklace, with the family; they had since he'd left his house that morning and throughout his whole journey. What if they wouldn't speak to him? What if they didn't live there any more?

What if they were dead?

His eyes searched along the houses. Looking for the right one. Still following the car in front.

Then he saw it, his eyes rested on it.

He sighed.

But in front of him and around him, with no warning, everything flashed white.

(•HAPTER THIRTY-FIVE

Again I was out walking alone and again I questioned why, as I walked down the dusty streets, with the broken-down cars, the blown-out shop fronts, the dark marks on the paths where someone had been hurt, and the buildings falling down, why I was still alive.

I was covered at least, I thought, and as always, it seemed all females I saw were. I walked the usual way back home, down the usual streets, with the faces of some shopkeepers I still recognised. For so long I had lived with what-ifs and if-onlys; what if Mama hadn't gone missing, what if Papa hadn't got that job, what if I hadn't given that money for Aziz's ransom; if only I could be with my soldier again, if only I could've left the country, if only we could find peace. But now at least, I could see a sliver of hope; the prospect of university, of changing my life, of a different future.

I thought of the future I wanted. To see Layla and her family, for Aziz to recover, Hana and the boys to be happy, visit friends from school and uni, talk to my teachers. To study, to learn, to aspire.

To walk along the banks of the Tigris with the sun on my back, to watch its rays dancing on the surface of the water. To see the monuments and the mosques and the churches in peace time. To see Tahrir Square free from soldiers. Karada Street with no more tanks. The skies no longer filled with the moaning of generators, instead flowing with sounds of the muezzin reciting the call to prayer, cars and trucks busying along the roads, making their way to work.

I wanted to hear birdsong not bombs, laughter not gunfire.

See smiles not fear.

Simple things, because everything else was beyond dreams, beyond imagination. Everything else rested beyond hope.

I closed my eyes and thought of a dream I had. In my dream I see Papa and me, walking down the street. I'm dressed in trousers and a shirt, nothing covering my hair. We stop at a bookshop and peer through the window.

Papa spots some history book and begins telling me about it. He tells me stories of Nebuchadnezzar as we stroll along. We stop for a drink. We sit outside and watch people going about their business.

We chat, we drink, we smile.

We see someone we know and they smile and throw us a wave. We talk about the trials of Iraq, its history, its architecture, its kings and rulers.

And their demise.

In my dream there are no troops, no soldiers, no planes overhead, no tanks, no guns. No regime.

We chat, we drink, we smile. We walk home.

In my dream.

But I know that will never happen. No matter how much I dream it. No matter how much I wish it.

And I know I will never again see Steve, that we had no way forward, but what we did have, what we shared for that short time, helped me through the worst of times. And for that I will always be grateful. For that I will always remember him.

I turned the corner into my street with my head down, watching my feet, trying not to trip. I thought about going to see Layla.

I looked up. In front of me the landscape was different.

My head started to spin; I was confused, I couldn't make sense of what I was seeing. Still my feet kept moving me forwards.

There was space. Space that shouldn't be there. I looked for my house, my home; the painted walls, the bougainvillea in the garden that Papa had planted, the blinds at the window, the rotting wooden gateposts, I could see them all in my head, in my memory.

I closed my eyes and opened them again, but still the scene was the same.

A car burning, flames leaping and roaring into the sky. Next to it, was that my house, my home? As my eyes tried to make sense of what they could see, I made out one gatepost sticking up in the air, marking the spot; the rest a ruin, a bomb-site. And I ran, pulled up my skirt and ran, to this pile of broken walls, a cemetery of rubble headstones marking my belongings below, a reminder of the lives that had gone on there. Our lives.

I pulled off my niqab, sat on the rubble and cried. One side of my house missing, in a pile at my feet, the rest threatening to fall, all the insides on display to whoever strolled past. A car bomb, I guessed.

My home was gone. And I didn't care who saw me, or what I looked like. I didn't care if the American troops, or the fundamentalists, or Al-Qaeda, or the militants, the insurgents, the terrorists, Sunnis, Shias, Christians, Clerics, Ba'athists, or anyone saw me, shot me, tortured me. I didn't care who had done it, who had destroyed my house, my childhood and my memories, the place where Mama still lived in my head, where I had last seen Papa.

Who did it? What the hell did it matter?

I hated the war. I hated them all.

I used to know what I thought of it. At the beginning I felt hope for a better life, grateful that Iraq would finally be freed. Its people would be safe. Things that happened to Mama wouldn't happen again to anyone else.

I cried and cried as I sat on that rubble. *It's only a house,* I told myself. *It's only a house. Thank God no one was in it.*

I scrabbled around in the remnants of my broken home, pulling up lumps of concrete and rubble, old walls, smashed furniture, throwing them to one side. *It was only a house,* I repeated in my head.

I looked through my blurred eyes, down the street empty of people, the sun at its highest, beating down, and I looked back, turning around to see what remained of my home. I wondered where Layla was, and her family.

Why they hadn't come out to see what had happened. And as I turned around, squinting against the sun, I saw the silhouette of a man standing close by.

I wiped my face and lifted a hand to shade my eyes.

A man was walking towards me.

Dust and dirt covered him, scratches on his face, his fingers bleeding, one hand in his pocket, his eyes flitting this way and that, glancing to the house, to me, to the car, down the street.

"Were you in that car?" I asked, amazed that anyone could've survived.

But he shook his head and pointed across the road to a different one, the windscreen blown out, bits of metal, lumps of earth across the bonnet and roof.

I didn't move. I just watched him edge towards me. And I didn't move away as he neared, I didn't shout, I didn't try to run. I just sat and waited for him. And he sat down next to me.

"I'm looking for Joseph," he said. "Joe?"

My thoughts paused for a second, then a million thoughts and questions flooded in. What was he, this man? Police? Soldier? Colleague? Friend? Didn't everyone know Papa was dead?

I knew I should be scared of him, but the more I

watched him, the more nervous he seemed. And I thought of how I looked, sat on the floor; my legs on view, my head uncovered, my hair flying around, my face streaked with dirt and tears.

"Was this his house?" he asked.

Despite myself, I nodded, drawing the dark cloth over my bare legs.

He sighed. "Is he dead?"

"Who are you?" I asked.

"I have something for him. Something I was asked to pass on. For Joseph Rassam, lives down this street, has a daughter called Lina."

I caught my breath and felt my face flush. I struggled to my feet, shocked, wanting to escape now, run away, back to my Auntie Hana, scared of what was to come.

"Are you Lina?" He followed me as I moved away.

I didn't answer.

He looked around nervously, then drew his hand from his pocket, his palm cupped around something. I saw it catch the light, saw a gold chain drip from his fingers.

"I was asked to give him this." He lifted it by the chain, and the green stone with the filigreed gold hung in the air, the sunlight glinting off it.

CHAPTER THIRTY-SIX

I felt my jaw drop, felt my stomach lurch, my breath disappear, my head spin. I stared at it, turning slowly one way, then the other, a gleam of colour against the beige city.

The colour of her eyes.

How many years was it since I had seen that necklace? Six now? Nearly seven? I remembered Papa's story about it, I remembered the photograph of the three of us together, the necklace dangling around Mama's neck, resting on her chest. I had never seen her without it, nor it without her.

"Where did you get that?" I breathed, my chest stuttering, my head swimming as I moved towards him. "Where did you get it?" I ordered.

He took a step back. "I was given it."

"Liar," I spat.

"No, no, no. I was given it. She asked me to take it, she asked me to bring it here, to Joe. She asked me to give it to Joe."

Tears streamed down my face. I knew what this meant. "Who did?" I shouted, staring at his face, at his mouth, his lips, hoping and praying that they didn't form the words that I didn't want to hear. "Who asked you?"

He stared at me.

"Who did?" I screamed, stepping towards him, my face close to his, ordering him.

"Sacha. Her name was Sacha."

I fell to my knees and everything spun around me, this man, the house, the street, the city, flew around me.

✤

When I woke, I was lying in my garden, on a small piece of clear earth on the other side of the house. As my eyes drew into focus, I saw a red petal from the bougainvillea squashed under a pile of stones, and for a second, before reality and memory kicked in, I marvelled over it.

And next to it lay the necklace; Mama's necklace, green stone, filigreed gold. I sat up. The man was close by, his back against what remained of our kitchen wall.

"You passed out," he said. "I carried you over to the shade. I hope you don't mind."

I shook my head and I lifted the necklace from the floor and rested it in my palm. I don't think I had ever held it before. I ran my fingers around the edge, along the gold, then on to the stone, feeling the smoothness of it, the coolness. I imagined Mama doing the same. And I stared into it, all the hints of colours hidden inside, a sliver of orange, a line of black, a speckle of gold; it was like staring into Mama's eyes, into her soul.

"I'm sorry," he whispered.

I looked at him through my tears, yet with a sense of relief in my heart. Had I known this? Had I accepted this a long time ago? That really she was dead?

"It was four years ago," the man said.

I looked at him, astonished.

"I promised her I'd return it, and I meant to before, but..." He shrugged. "I don't know," he said. "I wanted to tell someone the truth. Tell Joseph, your papa, the truth, what really happened to her, but I couldn't while I was a soldier, it wasn't safe. I thought about selling it, because every time, *every* time I looked at it, I saw her face staring back at me, begging and pleading with me to end it. But it seemed so wrong. Soldiers shouldn't do that. They shouldn't shoot civilians, even if they are prisoners." He shrugged, pausing, watching my reaction, wiping the sweat from his brow.

"I didn't know what she'd done, or was supposed to have done. It wasn't up to me to punish the prisoners, or for any other soldier. But we were told to. To do the most horrendous things. When I met Sacha she was dying, hanging on, but in so much pain. And I couldn't do anything. I don't know when she'd last eaten, or drunk anything, and she was lying there in the sun, her eyes pleading with me, scars across her face and body. Maybe she saw the weakness in me. I wasn't a good soldier. She was trying to say something, and I bent down to her. She asked me to kill her. To shoot her. She gave me the necklace, told me to give it to Joseph and asked me to kill her."

He closed his eyes for a long moment.

"And so I did. I did what she asked me to do. Every time I looked at that necklace afterwards, I saw her, her eyes, searching through me, and I heard her ask that question, over and over, and I heard the bang of my own gun and saw her soul leave her eyes."

I listened to his every word, and every word I

believed. This soldier, this man, perhaps I should have hated him, for killing Mama.

Yet I felt relief. Guilty relief. That I knew, finally. That she was no longer suffering.

I was grateful.

I didn't think of all those years we waited, not knowing, still hoping, keeping her alive if only in our memories, because it didn't matter any more. It mattered only that she was free. At last.

I only wish Papa could've known.

We sat together in the shade of my broken house, the man and me, and he asked me about Papa, and I told him. I told him everything. About school, university, my friendship with Layla, about Papa's job, living with Hana, Aziz being abducted, about Steve, the money, and the escape I nearly took.

And he listened, he laughed in the right places, and he sympathised in others. And when the sun began to head back down, he insisted on walking me home. He would tell Hana and Aziz, he said, he would explain.

AFTER THE END

As I walk down the street now, I leave behind me what is left of my house, its crumbling walls, its broken windows, the glass littering the floor; a flattened wardrobe that held Mama's clothes, a fallen shelf that had supported Papa's books. But I take with me the memories, of my life with my family, I carry them in my head, photos inked on to my brain that I will never let fade.

So much has been taken, so many lives, so much trust, so many friends. And so much time I've spent waiting, for Mama, for Papa, for war to start, for the bombs to fall, for death to catch me.

For democracy, for freedom.

For war to end, for peace to come.

I walk home through the destruction and loss, the tears and the pain of this city, this country, and I see these people who I live alongside with their fear as visible as the torment in their eyes.

But there *is* hope amongst this madness.

And there *are* good people amongst the bad.

I know there are.

Because I've been lucky enough to find both.

And I've been lucky enough to see that flicker of hope burning brighter than any fear.

I raise my hand to Mama's necklace hanging around my neck; I rub my fingers against the green stone, the filigreed gold resting on my chest, and I feel her walking with me, and I feel Papa at her side.

I glance to this man walking next to me now, this man who tells me his name is David. And as I take a deep breath and lift my head a little higher, I wonder if he will have a role to play in my future. I wonder what future Baghdad will hold for me. I wonder what university will bring. I wonder what friendships I will find.

I wonder.

With hope, I wonder.